THE LIAR SOCIETY

THE THIRD LIE'S THE CHARM

LISA & LAURA ROECKER

sourcebooks
fire

Published by Sourcebooks Fire, an imprint of Sourcebooks, Inc.

P.O. Box 4410, Naperville, Illinois 60567-4410

(630) 961-3900

Fax: (630) 961-2168

teenfire.sourcebooks.com

Library of Congress Cataloging-in-Publication data is on file with the publisher.

Printed and bound in the United States of America.

VP 10 9 8 7 6 5 4 3 2 1

To Stacey because you always give copies
of our book to your UPS man. And because we love you.

I t's happening. I guess I always knew it might. They're changing. We're changing. It's only the second day at Upper, and I already caught Kate staring at Bradley Farrow like he was a pint of Ben & Jerry's. And Maddie. God, this is so bitchy, but she's so much like her mother. She's always watching, assessing, searching for an angle to get in with the "right people."

And where does that leave me? My parents don't even know what a country club is, would lose it if they knew I snuck makeup or saw the way I hiked up my uniform skirt the second I walked into school. I'm lucky if they let me out of the house on the weekend instead of forcing me to practice piano until my fingers go numb.

I used to know who I was. I was the girl who wasn't afraid of anything or anyone. It was always my idea to sneak out. My idea to hide behind the gravestones so we could watch the Obsideo ceremony. My idea to play the game where we see how many phone numbers we could collect during one night at a Pemberly Brown dance.

And so I won. Every time. Until last weekend. Kate ended up with more numbers. I caught her deleting some so I would think I'd won again. It should have made me feel good to see her clinging to the past like me, but then I saw her smile at Bradley and watched how he smiled back and I felt myself slipping.

Slipping and sliding and becoming less relevant in this new upper-school world where most kids don't have curfews and the Sacramenta are no longer a dare, but a part of day-to-day life.

Kate and Maddie are growing apart from me. Everything is shifting. It's small for now, tiny fissures beneath our feet. But the fault lines are there and the ground is rumbling. Change is coming and it's going to shake up our world. I just hope they won't let me slip between the cracks.

Chapter 1

I missed Liam.

It had been two months since he saw me kiss Bradley Farrow. Two months since I told him I needed space. Two months since I started spending all my time with Taylor and Bethany in hopes of finally being inducted into their secret society, the Sisterhood.

Two months and I still missed him.

My finger hovered over his name on my cell phone. Maybe if I called him now I could make him understand why I hadn't returned any of his calls or texts. At first I was just angry. So angry with him for not understanding why Grace was so important to me. Why I needed to be the one to bring down all those who had a hand in killing her.

But the anger had faded and time apart provided clarity. It wasn't that Liam didn't care about Grace. He just cared more about me. He wanted me to be safe and happy.

It would be selfish to call him. Selfish to string him along.

Selfish to expect him to wait around while I worked on ending the Sisterhood once and for all.

Like a sign from Grace, the moment I put down my phone, the chanting began from outside my window.

"*In vetus amicus novus, numquam vinculum sororum refrigescet.*"
"New friend into old, the bond of Sisters will never grow cold."

I recognized Taylor Wright's soft voice, her words lifted on the spring breeze, floating through the crack of my open window. When I looked down into the darkness, Grace's pearls dangling around my neck, twelve girls stood like ghosts in front of the thick trees that lined our backyard. The breeze licked at the hems of their gauzy white robes, and each carried a candle, the flames spitting.

I eyed the phone, silent and still on my desk, and felt the pull in both directions. One phone call to Liam to explain myself couldn't hurt. Maybe that closure would be a good thing for both of us.

But the chanting outside was growing louder. My time was up. I had to decide.

Involving Liam at this point would only complicate things. I had to accept my official initiation into the last remaining secret society of Pemberly Brown Academy without any strings attached. And my attachment to Liam was long and tangled. There would be time to unravel our feelings after the Sisterhood was destroyed. After Grace was avenged.

Just as I was about to leave the room, my phone exploded on my desk like a battle cry.

It had to be Liam. It was a sign that I shouldn't join the Sisterhood. A sign that it was time to move on or at least try to work things out with him. Things had been a mess with us in the fall, and now it was time to choose Liam.

Grace. Liam.

Liam. Grace.

Liam.

But lately I'd begun to understand that the choice wasn't really between Grace and Liam. The choice was between grief and life. I could answer the phone, ignore the girls on my lawn, and go back to a normal life. No crazy societies involved.

I slipped back through my bedroom door to the ringing phone, to a new beginning.

But it wasn't Liam. It was Alistair Reynolds.

Part of me wanted to cry, the tiny part of me who wanted to go back to the girl I'd been before, the girl without some crazy vendetta against a secret society. I could almost feel Liam slip between my fingers, just out of reach as always. In his place was the ghost of my best friend, urging me toward the Sisterhood. And if I was being completely honest, I wasn't ready to let her go. Not yet.

I briefly debated ignoring Alistair, but I knew he'd just keep calling me back. Ever since the Sisterhood had destroyed the Brotherhood, Alistair's sole reason for being, he'd been more persistent than ever. He'd come to terms with the fact that the Brotherhood was dead, but that didn't mean he was ready to let the Sisterhood continue to rule our school. Alistair was one of those spoiled, little rich boys who instead of simply crying over spilled milk knocked over everyone else's glasses too.

"What?" I whispered, ducking my head as though the movement could soften the sound even more.

"Is that how you answer all your calls?" If there was some kind of Richter scale for how much you wanted to punch a person, Alistair would fall between one of those awful media-whore reality-television boyfriends with swoopy hair and a marf (man-scarf) and Ryan Seacrest.

"I'm kind of busy. Talk fast or I'm hanging up." By this time, I'd made it downstairs and could see the girls' phantom-like forms through our French doors. Thank God my parents slept like the dead.

"You've gotta meet me at the Heart tonight, Kate. It's important." I was so shocked to hear genuine emotion in his normally smooth voice that it took me a minute to identify it as fear. Alistair Reynolds was scared.

"As much as I'd love to hear what's gotten your Burberry briefs in a twist, I'm going to have to take a rain check." The regret in my voice was real. I still wasn't sure what to do about the girls waiting for me outside.

"Kate, I'm serious. I can't tell you on the phone, but you have to meet me. It's urgent. Life or death."

"I can't. I really wish I could, but I have a life-or-death situation of my own over here." I stood on my tiptoes and peered through the glass, wondering how long the girls would wait for me.

Okay, maybe it wasn't exactly life or death, but at the same time, it felt that way for me. I had to join the Sisterhood so I could end it. The wars between the Sisterhood and Brotherhood had gotten out of control. The secret societies had been vying for control of Pemberly Brown Academy since the '50s, and they didn't care who got hurt. They'd killed my best friend, Grace. And just because the Brotherhood had been wiped out didn't mean I was done.

And then maybe once I'd fought all my battles, I'd finally be able to fight one for myself and win Liam back.

"Look, I'm begging you." Alistair wasn't giving up. "Please, Kate."

"Can't. Bye." I felt zero regret hanging up on Alistair's pleading voice. There was no time and I couldn't afford to pass up this opportunity. And even if I didn't have initiation tonight, it wasn't like I owed Alistair Reynolds anything. He was a big part of the reason Grace was dead. He'd have to figure out his own crap like the rest of us.

I unlocked the door to my backyard and opened it slowly to avoid a creak, slipping through like a whisper before noiselessly shutting it behind me. I turned around to face my future, Grace's pearls heavy at my neck, the cold spring air filling my lungs.

This was it. My moment of truth. No going back now.

"Numquam sororis vocationi ignotum. Teneat manum tuam." "The call of the Sister shall never be ignored. My hand is yours to hold."

My tongue tripped over the foreign words, and my stomach dropped when the wind picked up and snuffed out all of the tapered candles in one swift gust of air. I was greeted with soft smiles and quiet murmurs of congratulations. They had no idea that a traitor was among them. My eyes caught on Taylor's bright blue ones peering out from beneath her white hood.

I was like a neon-haired Trojan horse, and they were finally going to pay for what they'd done to Grace. Eat your heart out, Helen of Troy.

Chapter 2

I blinked heavily to ensure that my eyes were truly open. They were. It was the darkness that pressed down on us as we soldiered through the thick woods that snuffed out my sight. I held my arms out in front of me, zombie style, to avoid losing an eye to a tree branch. I liked my eyes. They're kind of important.

The shift was subtle and I felt it before I was able to see anything, but I sensed we were at the end of our journey. The trees thinned and spread, and finally we spilled into the open, each girl stepping aside to let me through, forming a sort of tunnel.

And finally the ruins came into view.

The breath was ripped right out of my lungs.

I had no idea the place where my best friend had been killed was this close to my house. It was like someone had spun me around faster and faster and faster and let go, standing back to watch me topple right into Grace's tomb. You'd think that I'd have been drawn here before, pulled by some sort of magnetic connection, but I had never pushed through those woods before. I avoided the ruins of the chapel that we had all watched burn more than a year ago, just like I avoided going to Grace's actual grave. I preferred to remember Grace dodging bushes and diving into Pemberly Brown Lake in nothing but her bra and underwear.

Taking in the charred bricks and burnt beams of wood, I wished more than anything that I could turn around and walk back home. Screw the Sisterhood. Screw revenge. Surely my memories of Grace were more important than destroying the societies that had killed her.

I took a deep breath through my mouth, careful not to inhale through my nose because the smell of smoke would surely invoke a full-fledged, stage-five panic attack. As I stood at the edge of the clearing, poised to run, the girls' robes billowed at their ankles and their heads bowed one by one.

One of the younger sisters lost her hood to the breeze. Her long, dark hair danced in the wind. She caught my eye and smiled shyly. I recognized her as one of the first-years I'd seen tagging along after Taylor and Bethany in the hallways, and I knew I couldn't leave, I couldn't run. This girl trusted the Sisterhood. She trusted them with her life. She had no idea how quickly they'd turn on her if she fell out of line or couldn't keep up. She had no clue how little her life was worth, how little Grace had been worth to them.

And so I stayed. For Grace, for that first-year, and all of the future first-years who the Sisterhood would surely lure into its ranks like some kind of gold-plated Venus flytrap.

Reperi tua fata. "Discover your destiny."

The girls' voices nudged me forward to do just that. As it turns out, my destiny was hanging from a tree branch—a robe that billowed like a puffy white cloud against the night sky. I made my way toward the robe through the tunnel of chanting girls. When I reached my fingers up to touch it, the chanting grew louder and more fevered. For a second, my fingers faltered. I couldn't bring myself to touch the fabric, the robe that stood for all that I'd lost, for everything that I'd given up in my quest to avenge Grace.

I could still run. I could still change my mind. Go back home and try to be normal again, call Liam. But the decision was made for me when two of the figures in white carefully pulled the robe over my head. In that moment, choice was replaced by destiny. I reminded myself of the look on Liam's face when I told him I needed space. I tried to channel all of the anger and hurt I felt when he couldn't understand why avenging Grace was so important to me. I felt the robe flutter across my shoulders and float over my leggings.

Reperi tua fata. I grew more resolute with every slip and pull of the silk.

The breeze picked up just as Taylor cupped her hand around her candle in an attempt to reignite its flame and continue the initiation. She was the leader of the Sisterhood who had sacrificed Grace, left her for dead, destroyed the Brotherhood. And now she thought she had everything she wanted. She thought she had me.

Under different circumstances, the flickering candle and her cascading robes would have been beautiful. But my friend had died in a fire. A fire started at this very ceremony our first year, so to me the flame looked like a threat. A promise of tragedy to come.

"*Unum*, one," she said. The candle danced. Bethany Giordano stepped forward and angled her candle to Taylor's. "*Duo*, two," she whispered. Naomi Farrow was next, followed by the remaining girls in white. They each whispered their respective Latin as they lit candles, the glow illuminating the pride on their faces. I was last. *Sedecem*. Sixteen.

When my candle flickered to life, the girls raised their chins to the sky. *Memento vetus, excipe novum.* "Remember the old, welcome the new." I wondered if they'd added the line to remember Grace. Probably not. Taylor gathered every candle together. As each touched the next, the flame became one, growing, feeding off the previous candle. If the hot wax dripping down on her hand burned, she didn't show it.

Taylor's crystal-blue eyes met mine for a beat before she breathed deeply and blew the candles out. A line of smoke twisted upward. I had to choke back a dry heave as the scent wound its way into my nose.

And I was in.

"Congratulations!" Taylor tore off her hood and pulled me in for a hug, the gesture so jarring and unexpected that I almost forgot about the bile in my throat. "Let's celebrate!"

The girls scattered to set up a party, pulling food and drinks from bags that had been set out beforehand. Music thumped and laughter punctuated the end of one song or the beginning of another. The only thing missing was a campfire and a beach. Even as girl after girl approached me to say congratulations, my legs twitched and my fingers dug into the soft earth, my body still poised to launch myself back to the safety of my house.

"I know it must be hard." Naomi's voice startled me, and I was on my feet in a flash. "I've told them a million times we need to stop coming here." She kicked a charred piece of wood with the toe of her shoe.

"I just…I had no idea." It was the truth. I had no idea about how close this was to my house. I had no idea that in spite of the ruins, in spite of the flames and the smoke, I'd actually be able to force myself to go through with this. I had no idea.

"It's almost like they've forgotten it even happened, you know?" Naomi's voice was barely above a whisper and she looked around nervously, scared that someone might overhear.

"Yeah, I know."

"Sometimes being here, I just wonder if maybe there's a way that we could honor her. Make it so she didn't die for nothing."

"You're kidding, right? You think there's any possible way to make Grace's death okay?" My voice was shrill and loud. I couldn't help it.

"Shhh…they'll hear." Naomi backed away from me slowly, regret written all over her face. "That's not how I meant it at all. I just… there's bigger stuff going on here, you know?"

It almost sounded like she might share my goal of destroying the Sisterhood. Bradley Farrow, the former leader of the Brotherhood, was her brother, after all. But before I could respond, she disappeared into the woods. Naomi Farrow was either my biggest enemy or my closest ally. Something told me it wasn't going to be easy to determine which.

I wove my way through the clusters of girls. Quiet. Listening. Trying to get my bearings, collect information.

I paused near Bethany Giordano whose back faced me, her body hunched toward the thick trees and whatever else lay beyond.

"...Need to be disabled...already in place...Brotherhood... eliminated."

I could barely hear over the music but I recognized Dorothy Bower's sharp voice drifting out from Bethany's phone. Formerly Ms. D., PB's badass security guard, Dorothy now went by "Headmistress Bower," and despite her more powerful position, she maintained serious ties to the Sisterhood. After the Brotherhood was overthrown, the Sisterhood managed to secure Ms. D. the headmistress position at the start of the spring term.

Our previous headmaster, Mr. Sinclair, and I weren't exactly BFFs, but as faculty leader of the Sisterhood, Ms. D. stood for everything that was wrong with PB. Oh, and she was one of the only adults I'd ever trusted until she lied to me and manipulated me to get the Sisterhood back in power. Minor detail.

Bethany looked up before I could walk closer and catch any more words. "Hey, Kate," she purred. Her voice was raspy like she'd smoked a pack of cigarettes and spent the entire night screaming conversations in some dirty bar. "I don't think I congratulated you yet." She swiped off the phone, cutting Ms. D.'s voice in half. "So…congratulations." Her smile pulled at all the wrong places.

"Thanks." My voice held the sick sweetness of sugar-free syrup. Hopefully you catch more flies with aspartame. "I'm so glad we're Sisters now. You can tell me all your secrets." I gave her a hard, "playful" punch on the shoulder.

Bethany rubbed the place where my small fist had bitten into her arm. "Ooh, you're so right. In fact, I've got a secret for you already." She bent down and put her mouth to my ear. "You can cover up your nasty hair with a white hood and you can say all the right things in Latin, but you'll never be a real Sister."

She said it to hurt me. She couldn't have known it was exactly what I needed to hear. I repeated the words in my head.

I'll never be a real Sister.

Chapter 3

I woke up the next morning to sunshine and the grinding buzz of my phone vibrating on my nightstand. I slapped at the phone to silence it and pulled my thick, down comforter back over my head.

It had been after 4 a.m. when I finally got back home last night, and already the choice I'd made felt scarier, more real in the light of day. Parading around with the Sisterhood at night was one thing, but the idea of joining their ranks in the halls of Pemberly Brown on Monday made me burrow deeper into the safety of my bed. At least for the weekend.

My phone buzzed again. It was probably Seth, my neighbor who doubled as bodyguard, lap dog, or best friend, depending on the day. He'd want details of last night. Excruciating details that he'd be able to write about on his weirdo conspiracy-theory, secret-society-obsessed blog. I needed an IV drip of caffeine before I'd be ready to deal with any of it.

Or maybe it was Liam.

I'd already been over hundreds of different scenarios in my head.

Me: Hi, Liam.

Liam: Hi, Kate.

Me: I miss you.

Liam: I miss you too.

Me: Let's get back together.

Liam: Awesome. So you're done with that whole obsessive revenge thing? Whoo-hoo!

Me: Um, yeah, about that…

Liam: *Click*

There's a version where he asks me to marry him, a version where he drives to my house and tries to whisk me away to Paris for a romantic weekend, and my personal favorite, a version where he decides to get my likeness tattooed on his chest, radioactive hair and all.

But every fantasy ends the same way—Liam wanting something I can't give him.

Reality really sucks sometimes.

I threw the covers off and kicked myself out of bed in one quick motion. I wasn't sure if it was yet another Liam fantasy or my craving for coffee that got me out of bed. Did it really matter? Either way, I was up.

I snatched my phone off the nightstand and headed into the bathroom to brush my teeth.

Thirty-four missed calls. Jesus. Seth must be on a mission. I began scrolling through the names after I stuck the toothbrush in my mouth.

Seth cell (4)

Maddie (1)

Naomi (2)

Seth home (3)

Alistair (21)

My eyes widened as I scrolled through an almost endless list of missed calls from Alistair. Twenty-one calls. Whoa. It's not like he and I were besties. I didn't even realize he had my number before last night. I had totally forgotten that he called, and even if I hadn't, there was no way I would have called him back. It had been so late and it just didn't seem important. I took a gulp of water, wiped my mouth on my sleeve, and dialed his number.

One, two, three, four, five rings.

"Yo, it's Alistair..."

Voicemail.

I thought about leaving a message but hung up. It couldn't have been that important if he hadn't bothered to pick up his phone. I headed downstairs to find my parents sitting at the table with matching coffee mugs and vacant stares.

They both straightened up and exchanged a meaningful look when they saw me walk into the kitchen. Shit. I was in trouble. I had to be. They never lounged around in robes on the weekend. If they weren't volunteering or starting some house project, they were buried in notes preparing for some epic case that would require as many hours as they could possibly bill in a week.

"Um, good morning…" I moved as quickly as I could to grab a coffee mug and filled it to the brim. Something told me this conversation would require a major caffeine buzz.

My mother's arms were around me before I could even turn back around. "Oh Kate, honey. I'm so sorry."

"Um, hey…wow…" My voice was still light, but a pit began to form in my stomach, small, hard, and impossible to ignore. "What's going on?" My mind flashed to all the missed calls on my phone.

"Oh God, you don't know." My mother pulled back and rested her hands on my shoulders. "It's Alistair Reynolds."

The pit in my stomach grew until it felt like I'd swallowed a softball.

"Alistair? What about him?" I raised my hands and took a step back from my mother, watching her expression carefully. The slack muscles around her mouth and the way she closed her eyes and took a deep breath told me everything I needed to know.

"There was an accident, honey." My father's voice was calm. Unemotional. If I hadn't seen the way his jaw clenched and twitched, I might have believed that everything was going to be okay, but instead, the now basketball-sized lump was caught in my throat. I dropped the steaming coffee, hot liquid splattering on my bare legs, shards of glass biting into my feet, as I ran back upstairs. Back to my phone.

I swiped Alistair's name again.

One, two, three, four, five.

"Yo, it's Alistair…"

I hung up and redialed.

One, two, three, four, five.

"Yo, it's Alistair…"

The next time, I stopped listening to the rings and began counting. I watched the timer tick through the seconds and counted just like I'd done after Grace. Only this time as the phone rang, I stared at Alistair's face and counted.

Twenty-nine. Thirty. Thirty-one.

"Yo, it's Alistair…"

I paced back and forth in my room, calling over and over again only to hear the same stupid message. By the time my parents managed to unlock my door, I was on my twenty-first call. The exact number of times that he'd tried to call me last night.

"He's gone, Kate. It happened last night around 3 a.m. We didn't find out until this morning. I'm so sorry, sweetie."

I pushed past her, locked myself in the bathroom, and dialed one more time, staring at Alistair's straight nose and wavy hair.

Twenty-nine. Thirty. Thirty-one.

This time, I left a message.

"I'm sorry," I gasped into the phone. "I'm so sorry."

And then I threw up.

Chapter 4

Y ou don't have to do this, sweetie," my dad pleaded for what had to be the millionth time. "It's too much. Stay home. Your mom already called in an absence. We've booked you an appointment with Dr. Lowen for this afternoon. You should see him before you jump back into things. He's warned us that losing another student so suddenly might trigger some pretty intense feelings for you."

I stared past his eyes at the curve in the road. He hated when I did that. Dr. P.—short for Dr. Prozac, as I called him—had spent entire sessions discussing the importance of eye contact. But I couldn't do it. Not today. I'd spent the entire weekend locked in my room, screening calls, trying to pretend that Alistair wasn't dead. Trying to convince myself that it wasn't my fault. But it wasn't working.

Alistair and I hadn't been close. In fact, technically I should probably have been happy he was dead, or at least relieved. He was one of the people instrumental in what happened to Grace. If he hadn't been there that night, she'd still be alive.

But he wasn't a murderer. Not really. He was just a stupid boy who made a mistake that ended up costing my friend her life. I hated him for it, but I hated myself too. Besides, Alistair dying wasn't going to save other people from being hurt. The societies were the root of the problem. They made people crazy. They made them do horrible things.

And Alistair was no different. But all I could think about was the fear in his voice when he called me last night. He had been scared. He had been scared, and I'd been too busy to find out why.

I had to get out of the house. I felt myself sinking back into the blackness that surrounded me after Grace's death, and I had to claw my way back to the surface or I'd be lost forever. I had to go to school and at least pretend to be normal.

"At least let me drive you." Dad physically moved to try and meet my eye, but it didn't work. I knew if I looked at him, I'd start crying for Alistair Reynolds and I didn't want to do that. I wanted to go to school, nod off in my classes, and pretend that everything was normal. I heard a telltale screech of brakes that meant the bus was turning onto our street. Thank God.

"I'm fine, Dad…it's fine." I forced myself to meet his eyes with my exhausted ones. He'd never let me go if I didn't. And before he could put his hand on my shoulder all dad-like or pick me up and tuck me back into bed the way he used to do when I was five, Seth Allen erupted from his front door like a volcano.

"I'm gonna miss it… I got it! Mo-om, I've got it!"

Seth's hair was already mussed and his uniform shirt half tucked in, which explained the "I've got it," as Mrs. Allen was famous for her drive-by tuck-ins. He rushed down his driveway, tripping over his neon white Pumas, his roller book bag flipping off its wheels. Seth was a hot, hot mess and I loved him for it. He shot my dad an "I've got this" nod when he saw me, and I wondered if maybe he really did. Seth had pulled me out of the darkness before, and if anyone could save me from slipping back down, it was him.

The bus screeched to a halt in front of our driveways, and we boarded with all the other humiliated passengers without licenses or cars or rides to school. My dad looked deflated through the fingerprinted bus window, so I managed a smile before we pulled away. This didn't need to break him too.

"So your mom called my mom and they're all worried about you with this Alistair thing and supposedly it's going to create a whole new psychotic break in your hormone-addled brain. Want to talk about it?" Seth asked as he slid a Pop Tart out of his blazer pocket. The noise of him opening the foil wrapper almost drowned out his voice, and I willed myself to be patient. The thing about Seth was that he never had an ulterior motive when it came to being my friend. He always just wanted to help.

"I'm fine."

My hand went to my neck, but I'd hidden Grace's pearls beneath my shirt. Normally I'd roll the perfect spheres between my fingers and count each of the sixty-three pearls as I figured out how to respond to Seth, but instead I clenched my teeth. Seth knew me well enough to know that the pearls meant trouble, and I didn't want to worry him.

"I mean, it's not like he was my best friend or anything." I failed to mention all those missed calls, the guilt, the way this whole eerie scenario took me right back to the days following Grace's death last year.

I looked around at all the other kids on the bus. They weren't crying or even whispering. Maybe this was all some weird rumor. Maybe Alistair would amble up to my locker and tell me my roots were showing and explain in detail how my undercover plan was going to fail in that charming way of his, and everything would be normal. He'd be super pissed that I hadn't returned his calls, but my nightmare would transform into a mistake and I'd be able breathe again.

The bus turned a corner onto the tree-canopied lane that led to our school. Pemberly Brown sat on a hill at the end of the drive, all red brick and manicured landscaping. Every morning, the school's refined beauty greeted me like an aging socialite with a restrained smile and a cupped wave. Ivy covered the brick, vivid green since the spring rain, and the first of PB's famous flowers were sprouting in the beds around the building. I reminded myself to walk through the gardens after school. I could visit Grace's bench and see if the crocuses had begun to push through the earth. They bloomed early, pushing through the snow even, so if you blinked you could miss them. I never did.

My stomach dropped when I saw a group of suits unfolding themselves from expensive cars in the visitors' lot. Men straightened ties and women shrugged into blazers as they gathered together before entering the building. It was happening. When I'd finally returned to school after Grace's death, I'd learned that with the loss of a student came the addition of all sorts of important-looking adults. Grief counselors, board members, administrators from the lower and middle schools, pinch-faced psychologists only Dr. P. could appreciate.

"Kate! Wait up." I'd wandered off the bus without waiting for Seth, who struggled with his roller bag. I didn't have the energy to inquire why he even bothered with it. Roller bags were discriminated against in all high schools, as they should be. Bus steps, flights of stairs, narrow turns, crowded hallways. They all stood waiting to kick Seth in the proverbial balls on a day-to-day basis.

"Sorry, I'll catch up with you later. Gotta finish calc. See you at lunch?"

Seth's face dropped, and it broke my heart. He was worried about me. Everyone was. I guess everyone should be. This hit too close to home. All of it. But I had to get to my locker; I had to push past the huddles of crying people. I had to shove through whispers and "did you hears?" and awkward, inappropriate hugs from teachers. I had to ignore the way my mouth watered in that just-before-you-puke-your-guts-out way and calm the heaving of my stomach. If I didn't look, didn't acknowledge any of it, was it really happening? If a phone went unanswered twenty-one times, did it ever make a sound?

I touched the bronze plaques at each of the stations I passed, letting my fingers linger for a beat on the cool surface.

The main entrance, Station 1. *Aut disce aut discede.* Either learn or leave.

The computer lab at the end of the hall, Station 4. *Liberae sunt nostrae cogitationes.* Our thoughts are free.

Detention, near my locker. Station 5. *Abyssus abyssum invocate.* Hell invokes hell.

My name was called, but it sounded warped and distant. It could have been anyone—Seth tailing me, one of my new "Sisters" searching for someone to cry with, one of the grief counselors who barely recognized the girl with the faded blue hair as the preppy brunette who lost her best friend over a year ago.

But my body moved forward in spite of the crowds and distractions, pulled toward some magnetic force who stood waiting at my locker, his skin ashen, his head lowered. Was I imagining him here? Had Bradley Farrow really come to school after the death of his best friend?

I heard my name again from behind me, the word pulled and stretched. "K…a…t…e…"

I turned this time, spinning in slow motion to find the source, and found Liam frozen at the end of the hallway, a sea of students shifting and flowing around him. It was just like all of my fantasies, and like in all of my fantasies, I knew our conversation was doomed. I gave him a sad wave, and when I turned, Maddie was a few feet away from me, her head lowered, her hands balled in fists. I hadn't thought about her, hadn't considered how the news of another student's death would impact Grace's other best friend.

She raised her chin, and her eyes were puffy and red, but despite everything in our history, despite the fact that she was the only other person in the entire world who could even come close to understanding what it was like to lose Grace, I couldn't go to her. It was as though she'd turned invisible, and I could see Bradley straight through her, his rich skin ashy and his golden eyes vacant.

"That's it?" Maddie whispered as I moved around her.

I had no idea why I was doing what I was doing or why I couldn't see her standing there, but she was right. That was it. Maddie's eyes filled with tears, and she shook her head and rushed away. I don't know if I was still angry or if there was something inherently wrong with me, but I couldn't bring myself to follow. She fell into Seth's arms at the end of the hallway, lowered her head on his shoulder, and I caught a flash of disappointment in his green eyes. Everyone hated me. I was losing them, letting the only people who truly cared about me go, and powerless to stop any of it. There was just something about Bradley Farrow.

A year ago, Bradley had been my first crush. A year ago, I would have given anything to see him standing in front of my locker. But things had changed since then. I didn't trust him. He didn't trust me. I wanted him. He pretended to want me. The whole thing was kind of a mess, but right now, none of it seemed to matter because Bradley Farrow was broken, and looking at him felt like looking in a mirror. His face had been rearranged by grief. He was still beautiful, but now he was more Picasso than Rembrandt, and I wanted nothing more than to slide his features back into place. To change him back into the Bradley he was before Alistair died.

"This was no accident." His voice was hoarse, urgent. "Someone killed him, Kate." He looked around the halls, ran his hand over his closely cropped hair.

"I know." My words came out soft, soothing, and I didn't recognize my own voice. "I can help." My fingers reached instinctively toward my neck and I tugged the pearls out from under my uniform shirt.

And I knew it was true. I could help. His face crumbled into something that looked like relief before rearranging itself back into the stark grief I'd seen when my eyes first landed on him, and I knew Bradley Farrow was the reason I came to school today. Maybe if I could fix him, I'd finally be able to fix myself.

Chapter 5

"He called me thirty-two times." Bradley's voice was barely above a whisper. "Thirty-two times and I didn't answer one of them." He turned away from me and swiped the backs of his hands over his eyes. "They're saying it was a suicide. The truck driver said Alistair was speeding and he just blew right through the stop sign."

I knew Alistair had died in a car accident, but I hadn't heard any of the details until now. The truth was, I didn't want to know the details. I didn't want any of this to be real. But it only took one look at Bradley's red, swollen eyes to remind me that no matter how much I tried to wish that this was all a huge mistake, Alistair's death was very, very real.

"He called me too."

Bradley didn't move his head. It was like he didn't hear me. I reached over and touched his shoulder, lightly, remembering how I felt in the after-Grace. Remembering how my mother's fingertips burned my skin when she reached out to hold my hand at Grace's funeral. Remembering the way I had recoiled when Seth tried to hug me when he found me sitting on my porch swing hours after we'd gotten the official phone call.

I told myself not to be hurt when Bradley's muscles tensed at my touch. I promised myself that I'd never invade his space again if he pushed my arm away. But Bradley let himself sink into me until his arms were wrapped around me like I was the only piece of drift-wood in the middle of a tsunami.

"Twenty-one times. He called me twenty-one times." I said the words into his neck, and I felt his shoulders shudder and heave in a silent sob as tears from my own eyes wet his uniform shirt.

People were staring at us. I could feel their eyes on me. On Bradley. On the two of us clinging to each other, barely afloat in the sea of students. I shot daggers at the kids who dared to meet my eye. I gently pushed Bradley away and took a small step back from him. This moment was too personal for the hallway.

"You wanna get out of here?" I remembered my dad's words this morning, how my mom called in an absence, how we could escape without consequence. It didn't matter; I'd take the fifteen demerits, but it'd be easier this way.

He nodded once, and I grabbed his hand and pulled him out the nearest exit of the school. The earthy, wet spring air greeted us the second we left the building. I took a deep breath and steered Bradley toward the gardens.

The small stone bench sat in the middle of a riot of daffodils and irises that were just beginning to poke tentative buds above ground. As usual, the seat was cool in spite of the bright sunshine, and the moment I sat down, I got goose bumps. I used to tell myself that the constant chill of the bench must mean Grace haunted it, that she could see the flowers and hear my voice. But now I wasn't so sure.

Bradley sat next to me and cradled his head in his hands, palms rubbing his eye sockets.

"The funeral's tomorrow… I wasn't supposed to come to school today, but sitting at home… I just, I had to leave." He let his voice trail off.

"I know." And then I remembered how much I'd hated it when people pretended to understand what I was feeling about Grace. "I mean, I don't know. Not really. But I remember what it felt like for me. After Grace." I paused and ran my fingers over her name engraved on the back of the bench. "It's going to be awful."

I remembered Grace's funeral in smells, tastes, and sounds. It was like I had gone blind for the day. Or maybe I'd blocked out her tiny casket and the hordes of students who had been there pretending to know her. Pretending to care. Instead I remembered the bitter taste of the cough drops my mother had dug out of her purse for me to chew on. I remembered the constant wet heat of tears on my cheeks. I remembered the grotesque, medicinal smell of the funeral home. I remembered wishing I was dead.

"How did you do it?" He picked his head up and looked me in the eyes for the first time that day.

"Do what?" I stared back. Willing myself not to cry. Remembering how much I hated it when other people cried for Grace when it was obvious they barely knew her, that their pain was nothing compared to my own.

"How did you…I mean, survive? I guess I want to know how you keep waking up. How did you get out of bed?" The palms were back in his eyes, rubbing and swiping the constant stream of tears away. "How do you even walk around with all of these people staring at you? All of this…"

I could have filled in about a million different feelings where Bradley trailed off. Anger, sadness, hurt, disgust, grief, depression. Loss.

"It gets lighter." I answered with the truth and regretted the glib taste on my tongue. "I mean, it never goes away. The feelings. They never stop, but it gets…I don't know…livable, I guess. Like when you break a leg, at first it's excruciating and you think you're going to die. But eventually after you've had time to heal, it kind of fades into this constant, dull ache." A faint breeze whistled through the leaves of the trees and plants surrounding us and tickled the back of my neck like cold fingers. "You never walk the same again, but eventually you do walk."

I needed him to know that he could survive this, to understand that eventually he'd see a pinprick of light at the end of the tunnel, and it would open up.

"He didn't even leave me a message. Thirty-two calls and no messages. If he was going to kill himself, wouldn't he tell me why? I was his best friend. He wouldn't…he couldn't…he would have told me something. I know it."

I looked at my feet, not knowing how to tell him that Alistair had left me a message, that I might have his last words on a tinny recording on my cell phone. "I…wait…" I unearthed my phone from the bottom of my bag. "You need to listen to this."

I pressed Play and pretended not to notice the way Bradley looked like he'd been punched in the stomach when he heard Alistair's voice.

"I'm at the Heart of Brown and I know exactly what I have to do. I won't let them hurt him."

Bradley was off and running toward the old buildings that lined the fringes of Pemberly Brown's campus before I even had time to switch off my phone. Back in the old days, Pemberly Brown was two schools. Pemberly Academy was an all-girls school and the Brown School for Boys was all boys. When they merged in the '50s, an architect redesigned and expanded Pemberly's campus to work as a coed institution, and the old Brown buildings had sat unused ever since. There was one building called "the Heart of Brown" that the Brotherhood had used as their meeting place.

I raced to keep up with Bradley's long strides, but his legs were trained, his muscles taut after years of lacrosse practice, and were no match for me and my riding boots. By the time I got to the building, the front door was already ajar and Bradley had disappeared inside.

I yanked up the collar of my uniform shirt to protect myself against the dust, and I followed him into the darkened hallways. At first it wasn't bad because I had the light from the door to guide me, but when I saw that the trail of footsteps made a right at the first hallway, I knew it would be nothing but darkness from this point forward, dust covering any visible windows, classroom doors shut tight.

I put one foot tentatively in front of the other, willing myself not to panic in the dark. My hand shook as I reached into the pocket of my uniform skirt for my phone. God bless the flashlight app. The light of the screen momentarily blinded me, and I felt something graze my ankle.

"Oh my God!" Something scurried off in the other direction, too fast for the glow of my phone. I wanted nothing more than to turn around and run back to the safety of the bright April morning.

But then I heard Bradley's voice echo through the halls. "Kate! You gotta come see this. I think I found something."

I followed the sound of his voice and the thin stream of light from my phone into a large, cavernous room down one of the winding hallways. When I finally made it to the door, I saw Bradley kneeling on the ground with his own phone blazing.

"Here, take a look," he said without looking up.

Bradley handed me a piece of card stock. The texture of the paper was butter soft. Scrawling calligraphy in bright red ink covered the front of the card.

My Brother,

Alistair, your bravery will be tested. You must perform a *Factum Virtus*, a feat of strength to prove your worthiness. Each act of bravery is a test as our Brothers taught us. Should you decline to participate, another Brother will be sacrificed in accordance with tradition.

We'll be watching. *Tenetur per sanguinem*, Bound by blood.
A Friend

"I don't understand," I said, handing the card back with shaking hands.

Bradley narrowed his eyes at me, which reduced me to three inches tall. "It's a Sacramentum." As soon as his eyes began glistening, he turned his head. "They used to use it back when they first formed the Brotherhood. Whenever a Brother was threatened, you had to be willing to lay down your life for him. You had to be willing to sacrifice yourself. They stopped doing it when some kid died on the railroad tracks trying to save one of his friends from getting kicked out after he was found with a Sister."

I had no choice but to tell him.

"The night Alistair died was the night of my initiation."

"So you're one of them now, is that it?" Bradley stuffed the card in his pocket and started back toward the winding hallway.

"No, God no. I'm doing this for Grace, to make them pay." I rushed to keep up with Bradley.

"Whatever, Kate." His narrowed eyes flashed. "You really think you'll keep that up? Just ask my sister. No one can resist the call of the Sisterhood. Not for long anyway."

Chapter 6

"Wait!" My lungs burned as I tried to keep up with Bradley, whose pace doubled my own. It was no use. He'd either have to slow down or shout back directions to wherever it was we were going. I was about to lose him. "Bradley. *Wait!*" I stopped, my toes throbbing where my boots pinched them, my head still cloudy from the dust and the note and the shock of it all. I swallowed hard and choked back ridiculous tears.

Bradley slowed and finally stopped too, his shoulders slouching forward under the weight of Alistair's death and my confession. I shouldn't have even followed; I should have turned back to school and suffered through my classes the way I'd planned. If Bradley was anything like me, he'd want to do this alone. But I couldn't just abandon him. Not when I remembered so clearly what losing your best friend felt like. I at least needed to say good-bye.

I finally caught up. "Look, I'm going back. You need time alone…"

He cut me off. "I'm sorry." Oranges and yellows and browns

normally swirled in Bradley's eyes, but today they were muddied and dull. "Don't. I need, I mean I can't do this alone. I know things have been weird after everything that happened." He ran his hand over his shaved head.

By everything I had to assume he meant the time he kissed me in the middle of the hall. And the fact that I'd kissed him back. The thing about Bradley Farrow and his lips was that they really didn't give you much of a choice. Especially when you'd fantasized about those lips since you were a first-year.

I wasn't really sure how to respond. "Okay?" It didn't even make sense, but it was the best I could do under the circumstances. This didn't really seem like the time or place to rehash my crush on Bradley Farrow. Particularly since I'd spent the past couple of months avoiding him like the plague. "So, um, where are we going?" I stretched my neck toward the road. It was quiet during the day, everyone settled into work or school or whatever everyone else settled into on Monday morning.

"Porter. We have to find Porter."

It was a terrible idea. Porter was Alistair's cheeseball younger brother, and the Reynolds family was one of the oldest and the richest at Pemberly Brown. They were also one of the most private. It was hard to get into the Reynolds family compound on a good day. A few days after they'd lost their eldest son, it was damn near impossible. Even for Bradley.

But that didn't mean we wouldn't try. We'd rung the doorbell an hour earlier only to be shooed away by some well-meaning relative, so now we were stuck stalking the Reynolds house from behind a bush in a bed beside the house.

"What if he never comes out?" I whispered, narrowing my eyes at Porter's front door. We'd watched lines of puffy-eyed people trail in, ill-behaved children bringing up the rear, stooped grandparents being helped out of cars and up the front steps. It didn't look like the kind of house you could slip away from.

"We wait." A bit of Bradley's rich color had returned to his skin, and his eyes had the smallest hint of gold back in their muddy depths. Never underestimate the value of a good plan.

So we settled in for the long haul. We saw fourteen squirrels, one random cat, way too many ants to count, got pooped on once by a bird, and shared a granola bar. And Bradley was right. Porter wandered out sometime after lunch.

"Psst." Under different circumstances, I would have made fun of Bradley for the "psst" but I let it slide.

Porter turned stone-faced toward the sound.

"Porter. It's Bradley." He still whispered, but this time he pushed up on his knees, emerging from the shrub and brushing leaves from his blazer. "And Kate." He pulled me up too, and I offered a hesitant wave. I had no idea what to say to Porter. I could lose a friend every day to tragic circumstances, and I still wouldn't have any idea what to say to a kid who'd lost his brother.

To say Porter looked pissed would be an understatement.

"What the hell are you guys doing here?" Porter looked back at his house, through the windows at the groups of people in black smudged together like ink blots. "My family…Alistair. It's not a good time."

"I'm sorry." Bradley's voice cracked over the word, and he clenched his fingers around the now crumpled card stock. Lines of red ink showed through between his fingers.

"Yeah…I know." Porter looked back at his house again, a silent excuse, and I knew he wanted us to leave.

"It's just that…" Bradley unfurled his fingers and raised his hand out to Porter. "I have this. You need to see it."

Porter smoothed the card and read the words, the wrinkles on his forehead deeper than ever. He handed the card back, his eyes filled with sadness, and asked us to wait. Only a minute after he disappeared into the house, Porter burst back through the front door, not even bothering to close it behind him.

He held an envelope of the same material as the paper. There was no return address or stamp, just one word in red. *Frater*. Brother. Bradley took the envelope and placed the card on top of it. The two were a perfect fit.

"Someone dropped it off Friday just as we got home from school. It was a black car, dark windows. Totally sketchy. I've seen it before. Parked at the end of the street or driving by slowly without lights."

"Did Alistair say anything about it?" Bradley asked, tucking the envelope and letter into his blazer pocket. "Did you even ask him?"

I'm sure he hadn't meant for his question to sound accusatory, but I could tell Porter was offended. His jaw tightened.

"Not sure if you remember, *Farrow*," he spat Bradley's last name, "but my brother and I weren't exactly friends. I asked him a lot of questions. None of them were ever answered."

"I'm…" Bradley began, but it was no use. Porter had already turned to the house. "Porter, come on." But Porter didn't *come on*. Instead he slammed the door.

Chapter 7

The roller coaster above us sat still and silent, as though a brake were pulled mid-ride, screams hushed, people plucked away one by one. I hadn't come here since before the park closed, so I only remembered the long lines and excited squeals of weekend visits, not the broken-down, overgrown wasteland that surrounded us now. The towering beams of the track surrounded us like ancient dinosaur bones on display at the history museum, and the paint on the bench we sat on disintegrated between my fingers like ash.

"I still can't believe they shut this place down." I looked across the small, sparkling lake that sat in the center of the abandoned amusement park. "My parents met here." I expected Bradley to snort or at least roll his eyes, but it was my favorite story to listen to growing up. How my dad thought it was a good idea to impress a pretty girl by riding the Tilt-A-Whirl more times than he could count. He said he didn't feel right for a week, but he got the girl. Apparently my mom couldn't resist a good Tilt-A-Whirl challenge.

I glanced over at Bradley, but his eyes were blank, fixed on some spot across the lake.

"We used to come here sometimes. Alistair and me." He stood up and started walking. I followed. What else could I do? "We were first-years when they shut this place down, and the Brotherhood staged all kinds of stupid initiation stunts here." He shook his head at the memory. "They got bored with it eventually, but we never did. There's just something about it here."

"Yeah, can't say I really see it." It just felt wrong to be in a place that should have been crowded with people on a bright spring day and have it be completely empty. The rides were all stopped in haphazard positions, like legs, arms, and necks splayed at unnatural angles. There were too many places to hide and all kinds of strange smells that whispered like ghosts of happier times. It just felt wrong.

"What do you know about the Sacramentum they referred to in the note? Factum whatsits?" I asked.

"Factum Virtus? It's a feat of strength. No one has done one in years. The Brotherhood banned them in the '60s when that kid got creamed by a train."

I winced at his choice of words, thinking of Alistair and his car crash. Bradley must have had the same thought, because he froze mid-step and his skin turned an ugly gray color.

"Do you know who was involved?" I pulled a Seth and kept the questions coming in hopes that it might keep him distracted. Also, couldn't hurt to get some more information. Whoever had sent that letter to Alistair had either wanted him very scared or very dead. Maybe they didn't care which. But we had to find out who had done this to Alistair. And we had to find out why.

"You know how that stuff is. More legend than fact. I always figured it was something the older boys told us to make sure the hazing didn't get out of hand. Whoever sent it wasn't a Brother, I can tell you that much. They're trying to scare us. Trying to keep us in our place."

I thought of the Sisterhood, of Bethany and Taylor as they walked away triumphant after I inadvertently helped them destroy the very boy I stood beside. When would they stop? When would enough be enough?

Bradley stopped in front of a peeling wooden sign printed with "The Big Dipper" in peeling yellow paint. "Come on." He grabbed my hand and started weaving between the old metal bars that led up to the roller coaster like a maze. I resisted the urge to swing my body along the bars as I'd done while waiting in relentless lines, anticipation bubbling with every inch forward. Now we could move freely, the bars containing nothing but air, and I wished for the lines.

By the time we made it up the ramp to the platform, we were both out of breath. We leaned over the edge of the railing and stared down at the remains of the park below us and the sparkling lake that glittered in the middle of it all.

"Kind of beautiful, right?" He nudged me with his elbow.

"Yeah, it kind of is." My hand still burned where he'd held it. His fingers seared into my palms. Looking out over the empty expanse of the park reminded me that it was just the two of us here. No one had any idea where we were. It would take them days, maybe weeks to find us if we were to jump off the ledge.

My stomach dropped at the thought. There was nothing between me and a concrete nosedive except a thin bar of metal. And Bradley Farrow's hand.

"Why would he have done it? The Factum Virtus, I mean?"

Bradley shook his head.

"It was his brother, right? The note said something about Porter." I considered the words in the letter: *A Brother will be sacrificed*. It was no wonder Alistair had agreed to the challenge. Whether he and Porter hated each other or not, they were still brothers.

Bradley dropped my hand then and turned away from me completely. I'd pushed him too far. I knew it as soon as I said the word "Brother." But if I was going to help Bradley, I needed to know everything. And I wanted to help him. I wanted to right the wrong of Alistair's death, and I wanted to do it for Bradley. And for me.

"Not Porter." Bradley turned to look at me then. The breeze kicked up, and some stray leaves left over from our long fall and winter swirled at our feet. "Me. The letter was referring to me."

Chapter 8

Y ou're late." Dr. Prozac didn't like to be kept waiting. It was a fact that I could never quite wrap my head around. I mean, he got paid regardless of how long I sat in that sagging chair. He should have been happy when I strolled in ten minutes late.

"Sorry, this was all kind of last minute."

"You didn't want to come today?" His brow furrowed in a way that was meant to convey an interest in my response.

I shrugged in a way that was meant to convey my complete disinterest in this entire visit.

"Your parents are worried that Alistair's death is going to cause you to regress."

Ah, the old pretend-to-lay-all-your-cards-on-the-table trick. A year ago, this might have worked. I might have trusted him. But this wasn't my first rodeo.

"My parents have nothing to worry about." *Yet.* I added the word silently in my head, but I might as well have said it. Even Dr. P. in all of his pomp and jackassery heard it.

"Ah, well, it's important to remember where you've been, Kate. You have come such a long way in the time we've gotten to know each other. You must let yourself feel, let yourself grieve, let yourself remember."

"Right. Got it." I gave him a little salute hoping that these were his parting words of advice. And I had to admit, he kind of had a point. Part of me had to go back to where I was when Grace died over a year ago. I had to go back there so I could help Bradley through this. And maybe there was value in going through it all a second time. Maybe this time around, I'd do it right.

"Practice makes perfect." I hadn't meant to say the words out loud. Dr. P. looked up from whatever he was scribbling on his pad of paper, took his glasses off, and looked at me closely.

"That's not quite what I meant, Kate. Grief isn't a linear process. It goes in fits and starts; it zigs and zags." He leaned forward and rubbed his chin. "Let yourself feel. Let yourself grieve. Perhaps even take this time to help someone else work through their own feelings. Learn to be a friend."

And just like that, my bizarre relationship with Bradley Farrow got the Dr. P. crazy-pants stamp of approval. His secretary already had my follow-up appointment scheduled and scrawled onto a white business card that she handed me on my way out the door, just like all the other times. But as I pocketed the card and pushed through the heavy glass door into the bright spring sunshine, something felt different. I couldn't be sure whether I was zigging or zagging, and there was no doubt the spring air was charged with a sense of change, but Dr. P. was wrong. I was *feeling* and I was *grieving*. That's exactly how I ended up here in the first place.

Chapter 9

The smell of the funeral home brought back a rush of memories. For Grace's funeral, my mom had forced me to wear an uncomfortable black dress that was two sizes too small. There wasn't time to buy a new dress, not that I'd have wanted to if there were. But still I remembered constantly pulling on the fabric as I wove my way through the endless line of people to pay my final respects.

I was actually kind of grateful for the distraction. Grateful that I could pretend that the wall of whispers that surrounded me was about my inappropriate attire instead of my status as the grieving best friend. As I made my way closer and closer to the closed black coffin surrounded by enormous sprays of flowers, the whispers clung like gum on the bottom of my shoe. My best friend dying had made me the star of the show. The queen of grief. It had been lonely at the top.

Today Bradley was the crown prince of Pemberly Brown's second installment of suspicious student deaths. But he was more of a supporting actor in this show; it was Porter who had center stage. Porter who stood next to his parents in a perfectly pressed suit hugging friends and family, thanking people for coming, the white of his eyes pink, stripes of blue slashed beneath.

The scent of lilies almost made me gag as I knelt in front of the casket to say a short prayer. I bowed my head into my folded hands and tried to summon the right words.

I'm sorry you're gone, Alistair. I'm sorry I didn't help. I'm sorry I never called you back. I'm sorry, I'm sorry, I'm sorry. God, I'm so damn sorry.

My breath hitched and I bit back a sob. I was not going to be one of those people who cried too hard at funerals. I hated those people. There should be laws against them attending any type of service. There were categories of grief, and when it came to Alistair, I was a Level 7 at best. Porter was Level 1, which allowed for a complete and total emotional collapse and which for a lesser person probably would have involved throwing himself on the casket.

But Porter didn't look like he was anywhere close to the brink of anything. He shook my hand firmly and pulled me in for a hug.

"Thanks for being here, Kate." He held me for a beat too long, my chest crushed against his. "He always had a thing for you, you know."

Alistair had never had a thing for me in his life, but I was merely an extra in this play so I nodded along, knowing that I wasn't deserving of any lines. Sure enough, Porter was already on to the next mourner.

I wandered back toward the chairs that lined the enormous

reception room and saw Bradley sitting with his head in his hands. Bradley was a Level 2 griever, so the other mourners had left a polite circle of empty chairs around him. I remembered sitting in that same circle of emptiness. Like living in a bubble. I walked straight toward Bradley and could have sworn there was a faint popping noise when I took the seat next to him.

"You okay?" Terrible question. Worst thing I could have asked, really. But Dr. P.'s words were still echoing in my ears.

"Super." The word was hoarse, like he hadn't spoken since we'd spent the afternoon on top of the amusement park yesterday. Who knows, maybe he hadn't. "Found something."

He handed me a folded sheet of paper without looking up.

"It's the article. About the guy who died last time during a Factum Virtus. It's old, but at least we have a name."

I started to open the paper, curious what I'd find, but a shadow fell over me before I could even read a word. I looked up to find Liam towering over me, his face a cross between concern and irritation. It was a look I'd come to know well.

"We need to talk."

I crumpled the paper. It'd have to wait. "Um?" I hated that I looked to Bradley for…permission? But I did. I couldn't help it. It was a split-second look, enough for him to shrug his shoulders in response and for Liam to shake his head in annoyance. Couldn't say I blamed him. "Okay."

I stood and shoved the article into my pocket and squeezed

Bradley's hand before following Liam through wall after wall of devastated people. He never turned back to ensure I had followed, and I knew if I didn't, Liam would stop trying. He'd forget me and move on for good. I let him lead me because I wasn't ready for that yet. When he found a bench, he lowered himself and waited for me to do the same.

"I know I don't get a say. It's not like we're together anymore, but that doesn't mean I don't care." He launched right in, the words practiced and smooth. If I hadn't known him so well, I would have missed the urgency in his voice. "You said you needed space, Kate."

I wanted to explain that most of the time I had no idea what I needed. Did anyone? But how could I admit that this whole space thing was making me more confused than ever? I focused on Alistair. Alistair was dead, and it wasn't fair for us to be fighting about space and who said what and who needs what. Alistair was dead.

"I can't do this right now. I don't even know what to say." I wanted to tell him I was doing this for his own good, that he'd only get hurt by me and I'd feel guilty and that the last thing I needed right now was more guilt, but I knew the fewer words I said the better.

He shook his head as though to say "forget it." It broke something inside of me to actively see him forgetting me, but I couldn't do anything about it. I couldn't explain to Liam why I had to help Bradley and why I cared so much about Alistair, especially considering our relationship when he was alive. I had no words for any of it. As usual.

"Well, good luck then." He stood and said the words more to the ground than me. They were filled with so many more words that Liam was too polite to say. I hated myself for pushing him to this place but knew there was no other way around but through. Plus, Bradley stood in the middle and he needed me more than Liam did. For now.

Chapter 10

By the time I opened the sheet of paper Bradley had handed me, I was back in my room. It was a photocopy of an old newspaper article. God knows how he'd found it, but it wasn't exactly groundbreaking information. The name of the boy who died on the train tracks was Andrew Carrington.

It didn't ring any bells, so it was time for my old friend Google. The results were cluttered with middle-aged men with thick dark hair. Not helpful considering that the Andrew Carrington I was after had died more than forty years ago.

I tried narrowing it down by Pemberly Brown, but that yielded nothing but a link to our school website. Super.

I guess I could have tried Bing, but everyone knows Bing is for wannabes, so I headed toward the only site that always delivered—Seth Allen's tree house.

My first memory of Seth was the day after the Allen family moved in. It hadn't even been twenty-four hours since the moving van left, but

Seth was already outside with a box of Popsicles and a tape measure, surveying the huge elm tree that sat in the middle of their yard.

"Whatcha doing?" I called out across the fresh-cut grass, my knees scraped from learning how to use the roller skates I'd gotten for my seventh birthday.

"Shh!" Seth waved a pale hand in my direction and manipulated the tape measure, muttering to himself.

"Rude," I hissed under my breath and started down the driveway on my fancy new skates. I had visions of gliding past my new neighbor, hair bows flying. I was sure he would regret being so rude to a future roller-derby captain. Unfortunately, I hadn't really accounted for how steep my driveway was, and once I started going, I couldn't stop. I was planning on doing my patented move of rolling into the grass and wrapping my arms around my mailbox, but before I could get there, I saw a flash of red coming at me full speed.

"Car! Car!" Seth collided into me, pushing me down onto the concrete, opening up all of the scabs on my knees and elbows.

"Get off me!" Tears filled my eyes. What the hell was wrong with this kid?

"I'm sorry, it's just, there was a car coming and you were rolling right into the street and…" Seth's green eyes searched mine and the tips of his ears caught fire. "I'm Seth Allen." He stuck out his hand.

"Kate Lowry." I ignored his hand and pulled myself up to a wobbly standing position. I should have thanked him for saving my life. My mom would have made me thank him, but she wasn't around, and this whole thing was just too embarrassing for words, so I started back toward my garage.

"I'm building a tree house, you know. Maybe you could come hang out with me when it's finished?"

"Maybe." I was already inside my garage and regretting ever trying to show off for the new kid. Grace was right. Boys were kind of the worst.

"Well, I'll be here. Right next door. Whenever you need me," Seth had called after me.

And even after all these years, even after all I'd put him through, Seth Allen had never once broken that promise. While I still thought boys were kind of the worst, I knew Seth was different.

As usual, I heard Seth before I actually saw him. He was a mouth breather, and even though I was at the bottom of his driveway and he was all the way up in his tree house, I could hear the air wheezing in and out of his lungs. I'd made the mistake of asking him if he had asthma in the past, which resulted in the longest conversation about breathing treatments and how a long-term diagnosis would impact his parents' insurance rates. I still had no idea whether or not he'd been officially diagnosed, but I did know the amount the Allen family paid for their annual deductible.

"Hey," I called up toward the tree house. "You got a minute?"

"For you? I've got three." Seth said the words through a mouthful of food. In all the time that I'd known him, I had almost never seen Seth Allen without a snack. "Come on up!"

"Seriously?" I made it a point to spend as little time in Seth's tree house as humanly possible. I thought of it as a public service. Someone had to make him understand the social repercussions of acting like it was still cool to hang out in a tree on a regular basis. So far my efforts had gone completely unnoticed.

"Arghshshmp!" I had no idea what Seth was trying to say, but context clues and extensive experience translating Seth's food-garbled sentences led me to believe it was probably something along the lines of, "Get your ass up here."

I climbed up the spindly wooden ladder, careful to avoid the rough spots of wood that had given me splinters in the past. In spite of my best efforts to resist Seth's tree house invitations, I almost always caved. He loved that damn thing too much for me to avoid it entirely.

"So, I need your help…" I paused midsentence as soon as I realized Seth wasn't alone. Maddie Green was sitting next to him. I was happy to see her. Well, happy-ish. She'd been avoiding me since I'd slighted her in the hallway. Or maybe we'd been avoiding each other. We were best friends once. A million years ago.

"Oh, gosh, um, I didn't realize you had company."

Was this like a date? Were Maddie and Seth dating? The tips of Seth's ears were on fire and Maddie wouldn't look me in the eye, but neither of those things was even remotely out of the ordinary. "I'll, um, I'll just come back at a better time."

"No, stay. It's fine. I was just leaving." Maddie stood up, but Seth shook his head at her.

"Anything you wanna ask me, you can ask in front of Maddie." There was something new in his voice. Pride? Lust? Love? I couldn't really be sure what it was, but it evoked the tiniest pinprick of jealousy in my heart. *I* was the one Seth always had a crush on. *Me.* It felt like I'd been replaced, and I kind of hated it.

Maddie sat back down and I was forced to start talking. "I need some help finding information about this boy who died. It's really important."

Maddie sighed dramatically. "I don't mean to butt in…" As soon as she began talking, I knew I wasn't going to like what she was going to say. In fact, I was pretty sure I was going to hate it. "But this stuff?" She gestured at the paper from Bradley that was crumpled in my hands. "It's not healthy. I know you want to help, Seth, but you have to stop. You're enabling her. You're helping her to dwell on a situation that is done, over."

I opened my mouth to remind Maddie that it was rude to talk about people as though they weren't standing right in front of you, but she got to her feet before I could say anything. Maddie closed the space between us and rested her hands on my shoulders. "You have to move on, Kate. Let the police do their jobs. Let all the anger and the grief go." She looked away, eyes shiny. "We're never going to stop missing her, but she wouldn't want you obsessing about all of this stuff."

She turned then, her shoulders slouched, waiting for me to answer or for the tears to pass or for something I couldn't give her.

And then she finally gave up and made her way down the ladder. I let her go. What a bunch of bullshit. Maddie just didn't love Grace the way I loved her. She didn't understand how important it was to stop this from ever happening again. She didn't know that Alistair's death was just history repeating itself. She didn't know anything.

I looked at Seth. He was torn. I could see it in his face. *New girlfriend or old crush. Your call, buddy.* I wondered if he was going to make good on the promise that he'd made to me in front of my garage all those years ago.

"Give me thirty minutes. I'll see what I can do." He snatched the paper out of my hand.

The smile came fast and big. "Oh God, Seth, thank you. Thank you so much. I can't tell you how important this…" He cut me off by raising one of his hands in the air. I stopped talking more out of shock than anything else. Seth had never cut me off before today. Not ever.

"You have to promise me that this is it, Kate. That once the Sisterhood is over and things settle down with Alistair, that you'll stop."

He had his hand on his hip like he meant business, and I knew better than to argue with him when he was in business mode. I nodded.

"Oh and Kate, just so you know, someone put something in your mailbox like ten minutes before you got back from the funeral. It was weird. They pulled out super fast. Just thought…well, I don't know. It was weird."

I started back down the ladder before Seth even finished his sentence. My house. My mailbox. My ears were buzzing, my entire body shaking with adrenaline. Something was in my mailbox.

When I pulled open the black tin mailbox at the edge of my driveway, I was sure that I'd see the same thick envelope that Alistair had gotten a few days ago. I could practically feel the card stock between my fingers. But instead, there was a neatly folded sheet of notebook paper lined with bright orange words written in loopy handwriting that I recognized almost instantly. Handwriting that had me falling back, back, back to the time of bike rides to Dairy Queen with pockets full of change we'd stolen from my parents' jar, poolside in bikinis, the waxy taste of Super Ropes licorice in my mouth. Back to boy bands and coordinated dance routines and outrageous makeovers during an endless cycle of summertime sleepovers.

Back to Grace.

Chapter 11

From Grace Lee's Journal—September 9

Something came for me today. An invitation. As soon as I saw that it was addressed with my full name, I knew that it was going to change my life.

Grace Ai-mu Lee.

No one knows my middle name. Not even Kate. I told her and Maddie it was Anne. Cameron was there when I got it. Not sure if he saw it or not. Hopefully he at least missed my middle name.

The invitation told me to wait. To tell no one. To find some special seal in the woods Friday during the Spiritus bonfire.

But I've never been very patient, and the seal was just begging to be found. I ditched the girls, although they didn't seem to really care. Honestly, they both seemed a little distracted. Part of me expected to see Kate at the seal waiting for me with an invitation in hand. We both love a good mystery.

But when I finally found the seal at Station 11, the old chapel, it was just me. I'd never noticed the bronze plaque on the ground before.

Dirt and leaves partially hid the antique-looking symbol. I have no idea how I missed it.

The crest looks almost identical to our school's except for the S at the center and a different motto below. Audi, Vide, Tace. *"Hear, See, Be Silent."*

I still can't believe that I saw it. I can't believe that it's real. The Sisterhood is real.

I had a favorite babysitter when I was little. Sarah Hartwell. I loved when she came, all blond hair and perfect makeup, dressed in pretty clothes like she was going to a party instead of babysitting for a loser nine-year-old. She'd bring magazines I was never allowed to look at and teach me how to put on makeup or talk to boys.

I never wanted to go to bed, and she'd let me stay up until my eyelids weighed a million pounds and were impossible to keep open. And when I lay in bed and begged to go back downstairs, she'd tell me stories. About a group of sisters who held the key to everything. They wore a special necklace and their only rule was to Hear, See, and Be Silent. She'd touch her finger to her lips as she said it. I remember her sparkly nail polish catching the glow of my nightlight. Shhh.

But then she stopped coming. My mom found a new girl who was awful. She just talked on her phone all night and put me to bed early so she could watch trashy TV without me ratting her out to my parents. I begged for Sarah to come back but I was ignored as usual. Eventually I just stopped asking.

But this one day when I was shopping with my mom, I saw Sarah.

She wore dark sunglasses and her hair looked dull and stringy, but I knew it was her. I rushed over to her right away and yanked on her blazer. She bent and pulled me in for a hug, and I noticed a dark scar that ran down one cheek. I knew enough not to stare and instead told her how much I missed her, how my new babysitter was mean, how I wanted to hear more stories.

"They're dangerous. The stories are dangerous," Sarah whispered.

My mom dragged me away without letting me say good-bye. I saw her eyeing Sarah's scar, but she didn't ask her about it. Part of me thought that had to be worse than people just asking the questions. The noticing and then the silence. If it were me, I'd rather answer their dumb questions. Seems like it would be better than letting them guess.

Anyway, I never saw Sarah again. Honestly, this is the first time I've thought of her in years. But I know there's something dangerous about these words.

Audi.

Vide.

Tace.

I need a plan.

Chapter 12

The muscles in my legs gave out and I let myself sink into the mound of dirt surrounding our mailbox, last year's mulch biting into my knees through my black pants.

Reading those words in her barely legible handwriting with the orange pen she never went anywhere without was like talking to Grace. The real Grace. Not the Grace everyone remembered. Not even the Grace I remembered. There was no silk screen hiding her flaws or opinions or all the stuff that made Grace, Grace. I couldn't believe that I'd forgotten how awful her spelling and grammar were. Or the way she obsessed about her stupid babysitters and tried to memorize everything about them that made them cool. I couldn't believe she'd lied to me about her middle name.

Tears rolled down my cheeks. Reading her words in her handwriting the same day we buried another Pemberly Brown student felt exactly like the time Naomi Farrow aced a tennis serve straight into my stomach. It took my breath away and left only raw pain in its place. I couldn't help but hunch over.

I wished I could call Maddie back, tell her how sorry I was, let her read, let her in, but she was already gone.

"Kate! Kate! Are you okay?" Seth shimmied down his tree-house ladder in record time and stood over me all wide eyed and worried.

"I'm fine. I just need information about the boy. That's it. Can you help? Please?" The tears shining in my eyes must have worked in my favor, because within seconds, Seth was sprinting into his house to get his laptop, squealing promises about online databases and friends from his weird online conspiracy club.

I started picking at the grass by my feet, just to give myself something to do. Something to focus on. I wanted to read Grace's journal entry again more than anything, but I was a little afraid that if I read it again, there would be something else in there. Something I'd missed the first time. I wasn't sure I was ready for any more of Grace's secrets right then.

And then his voice.

"I'm sorry about earlier." It was Liam. I recognized his beat-up Converse, the pleading in his voice.

Go away. Go away. Go away.

Every piece of grass I plucked from the ground was a wish. I wanted him to disappear. Even though he was still over three feet away from me, the scent of him met me—laundry detergent, a bar of soap, his cologne that had all but worn off.

"Can we talk?"

I didn't look up when he spoke the words. I couldn't stop smelling him, but that didn't mean I had to look at him. Because I knew that if I looked at him, I'd cry. Or cave. I'd want to give up everything and just be his. "There's nothing going on with me and Bradley, okay? I'm just trying to be there for him. It's fine. Really."

"It's not, though. I don't…I just…you worry me, Kate. God, is it so awful that I care about you? That I want you to be safe?" He was pulling at his hair again, and I shifted my attention back to my patch of grass. "If you would just let me help…"

Every muscle in my body tensed. God, sometimes his incessant desire to fix everything was exhausting. Liam never just let me be sad. He never let me make mistakes. He's a fixer. And I'm a breaker. No wonder we never worked out.

"I just need to be alone." It was such a stupid thing to say, didn't really mean anything, but I didn't know what else to tell him. I needed him to leave if I was ever going to fix anything else. Liam cared too much; he was too close. It was one or the other. I couldn't have both. And I'd made my choice.

"But…"

I choked on the tears. "Please."

I didn't look up to watch him walk away, but I heard his footsteps on the driveway and eventually the engine of his Jeep turning over in the street.

It was better this way. It really was. I needed to let him go.

As usual, Seth was heard before he was seen.

"Holy crap. Holy crap. Holy crap." I heard him chanting the words as he raced down the stairs inside his house, flung open the screen door, and sprinted toward my post at the mailbox, his laptop tucked beneath his arm.

Sweat was dripping down the sides of his face, and there was still a tiny smear of Cheetos remnants on his chin. I tried to ignore both of those things and focus on what a great friend Seth was, but I had to admit the Cheetos shrapnel was a tiny bit distracting.

Seth stared at me and wheezed for a second.

"Are you okay?"

"Yeah…just…." He wheezed some more.

"Do you have more information on the boy?"

"Yes." Wheeze. "That's." Wheeze. "Why." Wheeze. "Running." Wheeze.

"Seth, seriously…are you okay?" Now that I was looking at Seth closer, he seemed pale. Maybe this was more than just him being out of shape. "Let me go get your mom." I hated to involve Mrs. Allen, particularly when Seth had information on the death, but the last thing I needed was another tragedy on my conscience.

"*No!*" Seth sucked in some more air and the color started to come back to his cheeks. "I mean, no thanks. I'm fine. Really. It's just…" He opened his computer. "You're not going to believe this."

There was an article from an old newspaper on the screen, and this time there was a picture of two boys.

A local boy was struck and killed by an oncoming train near the Arthur Road tracks early Saturday morning. Andrew Carrington was 16 years old and was first thought to be half brother Richard Sinclair because he was carrying his wallet and identification. The mistaken identity was quickly sorted out by local police when Sinclair arrived at the police station with his parents. Carrington's death has been ruled an accident.

I stared for a moment at the blurry photograph next to the article. Wrinkle-free beady eyes and smooth cheeks, but the same air of asshole surrounded the guy in the picture, even at the tender age of seventeen.

"Headmaster Sinclair?" The computer shook a little in my hands.

"Headmaster Sinclair." Seth nodded.

I lowered myself onto the soft, green grass and stared up at the late afternoon sky, twisting Grace's pearls between my fingers.

Oh, Grace, Grace. What does all of this mean? Why is an antiquated Sacramentum suddenly starting again more than fifty years after it killed our ex-headmaster's younger brother? Is he somehow involved in all of this? Has he gone off the deep end since being demoted to security guard after the Brotherhood was destroyed? And who the hell is sending me your old journal entries and why? I silently sent my questions up, up, up into the sky.

I had gotten over my habit of sending Grace daily emails, but that didn't mean I had given up hope on my dead best friend. Sometimes I pretended that if I could just ask the right question, she'd find me the right answer. But so far I was shit out of luck, and today was no different. The only response was the soft thump of Seth's head hitting the grass just inches from my own.

"What's going on, Kate? Whatever it is, you've gotta let me help." His hand inched closer to mine, and six months ago, I would have been totally grossed out, but this was Seth. My best friend. Besides, he hadn't tried to kiss me for at least two months, and now that I'd seen him with Maddie, I was beginning to understand why. So when his hand grabbed mine, I knew that it was an offer of friendship. Pure. Simple. No strings attached.

"You've already helped more than you know." I squeezed his hand lightly.

I did want his help. I wanted it so badly. But I wasn't sure what to even ask him for just yet. I needed more time to get my head around this entire situation. Everything was happening too fast. I needed time to process.

We lay there for a while watching puffy clouds shift and morph in the huge Ohio sky. And for a minute, I closed my eyes and tried to follow Dr. Prozac's advice to just let myself live in the moment, to let myself experience the present instead of constantly getting dragged back into the hellish fires of my past. But Grace's words were like lead in my pocket, pulling me back toward her, back toward the truth. No matter how hard I tried to move on, she was there. And now she'd been joined by Alistair, another casualty in the silent war that raged beneath Pemberly Brown.

By the time I sat up, the sun had moved behind a cloud, and Seth was snoring softly next to me. I had to keep moving. I had to take action. My present, my *now*, was haunted, and I owed it to myself to put my ghosts to rest once and for all.

Chapter 13

I didn't quite know what to do with myself. There were only so many combinations of words I could plug into Google involving Sinclair's name and his sordid past. I'd read all the articles, examined all the pictures, saved all the information. It was dark. It was late. I'd have to wait.

So I paced. And my parents yelled at me to turn off the light. To sleep. They might as well have screamed at me to be normal. So I did what any other *normal* teenager with faded blue hair would do when there was entirely too much night left.

I decided to go red. Blood red. The color of revenge.

As I rinsed my hair, the water a watery pink and the strands bright between my fingertips, I felt whole again, completed by the promise of tomorrow, of uncovering new information with a new look. The shock of it all only added to the fire I felt in my gut.

The red definitely worked.

By the time light spilled into my room between my closed blinds, my hair wasn't the only thing burning. My eyes felt scratchy and deprived, my head cloudy with exhaustion. But it was time to work.

"You look tired," my dad said over his newspaper, trying to disguise a flash of wide eyes and failing miserably. I tried to tell myself he wasn't trying to sound like one of the concerned parents on an ABC Family show. "And redder." He tried to make a joke, but it fell about as flat as a bike tire with a nail in it.

"Thanks."

"No, I just…what I'm trying to say is that I'm worried about you." I looked over at him with his graying hair and his straight nose. He looked like the perfect dad. But a perfect dad wouldn't keep his eyes trained on the words in front of him. The perfect dad would know how to talk to his daughter, or at least know better than to tell her she looked tired.

When I sat with my cereal, he turned and looked at me. Really looked at me for the first time in as long as I could remember. My hands flew to my brand-new hair as if he wouldn't notice it quite so much if it was covered by my fingers.

"Kate, I have no idea what you're going through, but my guess is that it's not easy to see another student at your school die so suddenly and under such tragic circumstances. Talk to me." The look in his eyes broke my heart a little. It was the same way he'd looked at me after I skinned both my knees on my roller skates. The same look he'd given me when I'd cried my eyes out after I found out Grace and Maddie had a sleepover without me in fifth grade. It was the same look I caught through my eyelashes when I pretended to be sleeping in the days, weeks, months after Grace died.

I opened my mouth to say something, anything to finally make my father stop looking at me like that.

But I turned back to my cereal instead, shoveling a spoonful in my mouth. And his attention turned back to the paper.

"I'm fine," I said between bites. I'd said the same two words over and over again for the past year and a half. Two magic words that left no room for discussion, no room for feelings, no room for parenting. God, I loved those two little words.

My dad dropped the paper and brought his plate to the sink, let the water run as he bent over the basin, his eyes fixed on the yard beyond.

"Gotta go." I cleared my dish, sure that if I caught that look on his face again, I'd spend the rest of the morning telling him everything that was going on.

"What?" His head shook and his eyes cleared as though he'd been dreaming standing up. "Oh, right. Okay." He reached out to pat my shoulder. "I love you. You know that, right?"

I just nodded and rushed to the garage door. In spite of my parents' long hours and complete cluelessness when it came to my life, I knew my dad was telling the truth. They did love me, and if I were a different person or maybe even if I'd led a different life, we'd probably have some amazing ABC Family-worthy relationship.

But I am who I am. My life is what it is. And my parents are well-intentioned but mostly useless. I had come to terms with this a long time ago, and the fact that I was questioning it at 7:42 on a Tuesday morning was more indicative of my need for a cup of coffee than family therapy.

I made it to school and slapped the bronze plaque at Station 1 as I walked through the main doors of Pemberly Brown. *Aut disce aut discede.* "Either learn or leave." My eyes scanned the hallway for Bradley as my boots clicked on the dark hardwood floor to my locker. I couldn't ditch class again, but there was no reason why the two of us couldn't stop by Sinclair's office during Open period.

I'd debated about calling Bradley last night to discuss the latest development, but I just wasn't up for the conversation. Part of me knew he'd want to pick me up and go to Sinclair's house, and I was too tired. I needed more time to process the ex-headmaster's involvement. More time to try to figure out what it all meant.

"Nice of you to show up." Maddie's smile was forced, and her uniform shirt was once again pulled tight across her chest. She looked so much like the Maddie before Grace died, before she'd starved herself to fit in with the Sisterhood, before she punished her body for her role in Grace's death, that I had to stop and look around the hallway to ground myself in the here and now. She pressed her books over her boobs and worked hard not to mention my hair. I appreciated the effort, but it annoyed me at the same time.

"You look tired," she finally said. The comment didn't earn her any points, even though I deserved everything she said after the way I'd been treating her.

"So I've heard." I started walking again. Maddie followed a couple of steps behind me and I tried to slow down, but then she sped up. We were off pace, as usual. As hard as we tried, we couldn't seem to figure out how to be friends in the after-Grace. Grace had been the third leg of our stool, and now that it was just the two of us, we kept falling down.

"I thought I could understand what you were going through, thought maybe I could help this time, but you keep pushing me away and I don't know what to do about it. I'm just, I mean we're all kind of worried about you. It's just hard to see you like this…" She twisted one of her springy curls around her index finger. "I mean, I know I wasn't there for you last time. After Grace, I mean. And everything that's going on, it just… I don't know. It's like losing her all over again. Kids are crying in the hallways. Therapists are talking in homeroom. You know?"

I did know. But I also knew I couldn't talk to Maddie about any of this. She had no idea that I'd joined the Sisterhood. And after what they'd done to her, she'd never forgive me if she found out. Plus, she was totally Team Liam with the whole "Kate should stay the hell away from the crazy secret societies and learn to deal with her grief like a normal person" scenario. The two of them should get T-shirts made up.

So I had no choice but to "I'm fine" her. I wished I could grab

Maddie's arm and drag her into the nearest bathroom stall and tell her everything, but those days were long gone. At least until I'd figured out who killed Alistair and put an end to the Sisterhood. Surely, justice had to come before girl talk.

"Guess who, Sis?" a voice rasped from behind me as two large hands covered my eyes.

"How could she possibly guess?" Maddie hissed. This game was universally hated and only amplified with Bethany "Beefany" Giordano's paws pressed over my eyes.

She roughly spun me around. "How's my baby Sister doing?" Her sticky sweet voice was directed at me, but her huge brown eyes were locked on Maddie.

Maddie gave me a long look and then turned back to Bethany. I knew the minute she figured out what was going on, because her eyes got squinty and her lips went thin. It was the face she made right before she started crying. Without another word, she turned and began walking down the hallway at warp speed.

"Wait! Maddie! I can explain!"

"Explain what? That you're one of us now?" Bethany batted her eyelashes and smiled triumphantly at Maddie's back.

I closed my eyes for a minute and tried to collect myself before I laid into my new "Sister" and got myself kicked out of the stupid society I was trying to infiltrate.

"I was going to tell her eventually. You didn't have to do that."

"What does it matter? You're with us now, right? You're not going to have time for losers like her. Not with us around." Bethany looked down at me and gave me her most syrupy smile. While Taylor had always been eager for me to join the Sisterhood's ranks, Bethany was never quite so sure. She didn't trust me; I didn't trust her. It was kind of our thing.

After Grace died, I knew Taylor felt bad about what had happened. She was eaten alive with grief like the rest of us. But Bethany was a different story, and more and more it felt like she was the one pulling the strings. I knew it was her idea to stage her disappearance to get the Brotherhood kicked out. Taylor went along with it because she thought it was what was best for the society, but she never would have come up with it on her own.

And now, as if she was trying to prove that it was all worthwhile, Taylor was hell bent on creating a new and improved Sisterhood. And apparently I was part of her vision. I'm sure it was partly her guilty conscience, but I didn't care. Being a Sister was my only chance to end them for good.

Unfortunately, it seemed like Bethany was on to me.

"So, what have you been up to since initiation? There are all sorts of rumors flying around about you and Bradley."

"Can't believe everything you hear," I retorted.

"No, I just believe what I see. And I saw you holding hands at the funeral yesterday."

"Do you even hear yourself? Holding hands at his best friend's funeral isn't exactly a hot date. His best friend is dead and I might be the only person who has even the slightest clue of what he's going through, so yeah, I held his freaking hand."

"Easy there. No need to jump down my throat." Bethany raised her long fingers and pretended to cower in front of me.

God, I hated her. She was intentionally trying to get me fired up, and it worked. And now it was time for her grand finale.

"Honestly, the only reason I asked is because I'm curious about Liam."

I choked on air.

"Liam?" She had to be joking.

"Yeah, is he," she ran her fingers through her long hair, "is he, like, available?"

I rolled my eyes at her. There was no chance in hell that Liam would ever go for a girl like Bethany.

"Totally. All yours. He's a free man. Bet he's just been waiting for the chance to get it on with you after you told the entire school that he has herpes and blackmailed him for months about what he saw the night Grace died. Good luck with that, B." I gave her one last parting smile, slammed my locker shut, and started toward class.

"Good to know! I was hoping you'd say that." Bethany flipped her long hair and adjusted the books in her arms. "Nice hair, by the way. Wherever do you get your color done?"

But she didn't wait around for an answer. I heard her snicker as she walked away. Bitch.

I slid into my homeroom desk right before the bell rang. As

Verbum began, the morning announcements read by two kids I recognized from Concilium, I slipped my phone out of my backpack and sent a quick text to Bradley. Screw Bethany. I was on a mission.

1:12. Stacks.

I had a little over six hours to plan out exactly what we were supposed to do with this information about Headmaster Sinclair. Six hours to decide whether or not I should let Bradley hold my hand again. Six hours.

Chapter 14

The clock tower, Station 2, loomed ahead, imposing as it ticked past the one o'clock hour. Year-two students had Open this period, and the most popular loitered around the brick behemoth happy and loud, their free period slipping away with every laugh or friendly punch. *Tempus edax rerum.* "Time is the devourer of all things." Time always seemed hungriest during Open.

I loved the tower. The long shadows it cast on the green, the five-degree temperature change when you entered the darkened space. I made it a point to walk past it every day after school, and I spent a lot of time within its cool walls reading by one of the windows, thinking, or talking to Grace. But today I veered early. At the center of the popular crowd stood Taylor and beside her Bethany, and I didn't have time for them. It was hard enough to avoid Liam and Maddie all day. At the rate my people-to-avoid list was growing, I wasn't going to be able to leave my house by the end of the week.

Sure enough, I heard my name carried sweetly across the green, a slight question mark tacked at the end. I figured it had to do with my new blood-red locks.

When I turned (because you always turned for Taylor Wright), she waved me over, her white teeth catching the sun. She didn't even wait to see if I'd come, because everyone always came when she called them. Instead she turned, continuing her conversation, assuming that I'd be scampering over like her well-trained dog.

"I can't! I have a study group," I yelled over, referencing the pile of books in my arms for effect. A hush fell over Taylor's lackeys. Taylor's eyes narrowed, and she took a breath like she might yell something back at me, but she pursed her lips instead.

I just tucked the books closer to my chest and rushed nerd-alert style across the remainder of the green toward the Pemberly Brown library. Toward Bradley Farrow. Toward ex-Headmaster Sinclair. Swallowing back any nervousness, I swiped my student ID to enter.

I braced myself to see the ex-headmaster, totally focused on keeping my face impassive. Worried that he would take one look at me and know that I knew about his half brother.

But I shouldn't have worried. A new guy manned Sinclair's post. His security hat was pulled low over his eyes and he was young— couldn't have been more than twenty-five—and scrolling through something on his phone.

"Where's the headmaster?" I blurted out, hearing my mistake as the kid's forehead furrowed. "I mean, Mr. Sinclair. Where's Mr. Sinclair?"

"Sabbatical. Can I help you with something?"

Now it was my turn to furrow my brow. Sinclair had taken a sabbatical right at the same time another student died under circumstances eerily similar to his half brother? This was more than just a coincidence. It had to be.

"There you are," Bradley called from a table near the door of the library. His cheekbones were sunken, eyes puffy. Blank eyes met my questioning ones.

I glanced nervously out the glass doors to make sure I hadn't been followed and double-checked the security desk. The young kid smirked down at his phone.

"Please tell me you know what all this means. How the hell did no one know that Sinclair's brother was killed in a Factum Virtus?" Bradley asked.

I smoothed my hair, self-conscious all of the sudden about the shocking new color. Bradley didn't appear to notice either way. "I don't know, but it's related, right?" I kept my voice low. I wondered if I should mention Grace's journal page tucked away in my pocket. I could shift in my seat and pull it out, unfold the page and smooth it against my leg. Let Bradley read the words. I could. But I looked down at my fingers instead. I wasn't ready yet.

"What does this even mean?" Bradley asked again even though no one had the answers.

"I have no idea. That new security guard said Sinclair's on sabbatical, but Seth got his address. We can go after school. Maybe ask him some questions?"

Bradley leaned back in his seat and rubbed his fingers roughly over his eyes. He didn't want to do this. I could tell he didn't want to go there. He wanted last week. He'd give anything to go back to a time where Alistair was still alive. If he could stop his friend from taking the challenge, he would give everything he had. And I knew exactly how he felt. I'd still give anything to go back to last year. Back to Grace.

"Meet me at the arches after ninth." Bradley's eyes flicked up to the clock above us. 1:48. Open was almost over.

The arches. Station 5. Pemberly Brown had twelve stations that were really just random plaques on school landmarks etched with ominous Latin proverbs. The stations also marked the entrances to the underground tunnels. The tunnels that the societies had been fighting over for the past forty years. Whoever owned the tunnels owned the school. The Sisterhood had originally built them as a way to move about the school freely after the boys had invaded the private girls' academy. And now that they've vanquished the Brotherhood, the Sisters had the tunnels back.

"The arches?" My voice cracked a little. According to legend, if you kissed under the arches, Station 5, you'd get married. Nerves spread like a virus in my belly. It felt wrong to imagine anything as selfish as a kiss right now, but I couldn't help it.

"Yeah, but first follow me. We've got a few minutes left and I have an idea."

I followed Bradley back toward the front desk.

"Hey, man," he said to the security guard, who barely looked up. "I'm an office aide for Mr. Sinclair and I accidentally left my Econ binder in his office Friday. Mind if I slip in and get it?"

"Be my guest," the kid said, nodding toward Sinclair's open door. I followed Bradley in, amazed at his natural ability to lie. I thought I was good. We actually made a good team, and all I had to do was follow. Not a bad gig.

As soon as we were through the door, we sifted through piles of papers, moved books, opened drawers. Sinclair's desk looked like a hoarder's paradise, so we really couldn't do much more damage. I flipped through an old, dog-eared yearbook, marveling at how different kids from the '60s looked compared to our school pictures.

"Kate…" Bradley's voice had an edge to it that immediately grabbed my attention.

I waded through the piles of paper and walked over to where he was standing with a thin sheet of paper trembling in his hand.

"Look at this."

It was nothing really. Or it could have been nothing. Just a class list for third-years. Rows and rows of black names printed on cheap printer paper.

But it was the slash of yellow that caught my eye. And the name it highlighted.

Alistair Reynolds.

"What the hell is he doing with a class list with Alistair's name highlighted?" I asked.

The list was at the top of a pile of zoological records in regards to our school mascot, a wolf whose habitat was maintained on campus as a part of a new Parent Teacher Association grant. His name was Bondi, and it apparently took thousands of dollars a month to support his reserve. Fascinating if you cared. I didn't. The only thing I cared about was piecing together all of these seemingly random pieces of information to understand what had happened to Alistair and why, but it was like someone had mixed the pieces of five different puzzles together into one box. None of them seemed to fit.

"We have five minutes to get back to Main," I said, checking the time on my phone. "But I'll meet you by the arches after school."

Bradley tucked the files into his blazer and raised an eyebrow. "What? Oh yeah…the arches."

His golden eyes were dull and blank again. It was almost like he didn't see me, and I couldn't blame him. In fact, I knew the feeling. I imagined all he could see was his best friend's name, reduced to nothing but highlighted black letters on a piece of paper.

Chapter 15

I had to admit that there was a vague sense of disappointment when Bradley didn't grab my hand after school. So much for the romance of the arches. I did, however, manage to get some type of bug stuck in my eye. I tried to tell myself that it had nothing at all to do with my furiously batting eyelashes. Surely that was just a natural, feminine response to the hotness that is Bradley Farrow.

"You have the address?"

"5067 Longacre Lane," I said, trying to fish the bug out without smudging my mascara or causing permanent damage to my cornea.

Longacre Lane ran parallel to the main drive leading to PB and was still officially considered campus, so we walked through the gardens toward the road. Neat houses were tucked on the street, many inhabited by the families of teachers and administrators who worked at Pemberly Brown.

I didn't want to think about what we'd actually do when we found the house. Sinclair was dangerous. He'd had a hand in covering up

Grace's death, snuffing out every piece of evidence to protect the school at all costs. And now that Ms. D. had demoted him to head of campus security, he'd stopped shaving and started wearing sweat suits to school. He looked like Forrest Gump after he ran across America, only with crazy eyes.

"I'll ring the doorbell and distract Sinclair at the door, tell him I have to interview him for a project or something." Bradley rubbed his eyes. "Go around back and see if you can enter through a back door or window. Take anything that looks interesting."

Clearly, Bradley didn't have any qualms about putting my personal safety at risk to further our little investigation. Liam would have flipped his shit if he was there to see me sneak around the back of the house to do Bradley's dirty work. I tried really hard to convince myself that it was empowering, that Bradley and I were on the same page, both of us willing to sacrifice anything for justice. But mostly I just felt disposable. And a little scared. Breaking and entering into Sinclair's house freaked me out.

I remembered reading an article in one of my mom's boring home-decorating magazines that claimed a person's home represented its owner's inner psyche. If there was any truth to that BS, Sinclair's house was the spitting image of his identity. It was smaller than the rest on the lane, sitting on a large corner lot, all smug and proud. But the grass was wild and the flowerbeds overgrown, and tall bushes covered most of the windows. It looked like a house that had given up, a house that didn't have anything left to lose. It looked ominous.

I did my best to ignore my shaky legs and moved toward the back door, listening carefully for the ring of the doorbell, my cue.

Ding dong.

The back porch of the house was screened, and I held my breath when I tried the door.

Open. Open. God, Grace, whoever is listening, please let this door open.

Someone must have been listening, because the door slid quietly on its track and I slipped through like a whisper. The doorbell chimed a second time and my heart thundered in response to the sound, but I couldn't hear footsteps approaching the door, couldn't hear Sinclair's voice or Bradley requesting a fake interview. Maybe he was out and we could both hunt for information.

But as I slid closer to the window, I noticed something red along the glass, a gross swipe of jelly or some sort of candy. Ew. I hoped I wouldn't have to touch it as I crawled through the window.

"Ohhhhh." I spun around at the moan, expecting Bradley behind me in the yard, but no one was there. The sound had come from inside. There was someone inside. There was someone close to the window.

More jelly on the floor. Why was there so much jelly on the floor? Where was the broken bottle? I stepped closer. And closer. And saw him. The pools of red on the floor weren't jelly. Not jelly. Not jelly. Not jelly. I screamed as loud as my voice would let me.

Bradley sprinted to the backyard, the door slamming as he entered the back porch. His eyes were wide as he pressed his hands onto my shoulders asking if I was all right, surveying me from top to bottom.

"The window…"

Bradley pulled the screen free and opened the window farther, sticking his head in and gasping himself. "Oh my God."

Sinclair was sprawled on the kitchen floor, surrounded by blood. My eyes blurred at the sight of him, either with tears or as some sort of automatic coping mechanism to protect me from further trauma. I couldn't do this. I couldn't deal with another death.

But then I heard it again. The moan.

"Oh my God, Kate, he's still alive! Call 911!"

Sinclair's eyes bulged as we came closer and he shook his head, trying to move closer and closer to the door. His arms were completely covered in blood, and half of his face appeared severely disfigured. "Wooolf." He said the word as I dialed 911 and tried to explain what we'd found.

Bradley gently pressed towels over Sinclair's wounds and he moaned in response. "What happened?" he asked, searching the room.

"Wooolf," was all Sinclair was able to say.

"Five minutes," I said, placing the phone on the counter. I couldn't look at him. I couldn't look down. And then I remembered why we'd come here, how we'd thought Sinclair was involved. Maybe he was as much a victim as anyone else. Five minutes. I rushed into the family room where a TV screen glowed, odd shadows cast along the walls and ceiling. Nothing but a broken lamp and some dirt knocked out of a planter. I searched the rest of the first floor and found nothing but tipped furniture, evidence of a break-in.

Distant sirens rang out. The second floor. I had to check the second floor. I ran toward the front of the house, toward the stairs that would lead me up. And there, perched in the middle of a step was a note on the same creamy card stock as Alistair's message.

Part of an old yearbook page had been pasted to the card, bold words scripted in red over the faces of students.

Specta lupos. It's your turn now. Anni 1964. Page 17.

Faciem Lupis. Wolf. "Face the wolves." Save the Brothers. Year 1964. Page 17. This must have been what Sinclair had been mumbling about. I shoved the note under my uniform shirt just as the foyer was bathed in red and blue lights, and then I heard it. A sound so quiet, so menacing that I felt it in my bones instead of hearing it in my ears. The sirens began to wail, and for a moment, I thought I must have imagined it, but in the split second of silence, I heard it again. From the shadows. A low, menacing growl.

Chapter 16

Before my brain had even processed the fact that there was an actual wolf in Sinclair's house, I saw a flash of gray and white fur leap from the steps. My arms flew over my face, and I braced myself for the impact of claws and teeth on the tender skin of my forearms. Can you die from a wolf attack if you aren't a vampire? Based on Sinclair's blood-stained kitchen floor, I thought yes.

A sharp yelp pierced the air, followed by the dull thump of a body.

"Kate! Are you okay?" Seth stood in the doorway, a stun gun pointed in the space above my head.

"There's a wolf." Clearly the shock of my near wolf attack had left me with a new superpower for stating obvious facts long after they were relevant. Awesome.

"We've been listening to police radio all night. I just knew something like this was going to happen. Glad I had my taser with me."

I should have been hugging Seth or at the very least thanking him for saving my life, but the only thing I really took away from his little explanation was the term "we." Because "we" could only really mean one thing. Or one *person* specifically.

"Jesus, what the hell is going on in here?" Liam pushed Seth aside and only hesitated a second before pulling me to my feet and away from the stairs in one swift movement. He stared at me a second too long, taking in my new hair with sad eyes. His mouth opened to say something, but then closed again as though he'd abruptly remembered that we weren't on good enough terms for him to make a sly comment on my new look. A wave of sadness washed over me when I realized I wanted him to.

"There was a wolf. But I saved her. It's cool." Seth's face was bright red and he was practically bursting with pride.

Liam looked from the lump of wolf on the ground to me, and I nodded slowly. "He saved my life." And it was like hearing the words out loud suddenly made them sink in. "You saved my life. Oh my God, Seth." I wrapped my arms around him and squeezed so tight that I heard his spine crack.

He mumbled something that sounded like "I love you" but could have been "I saved you." I chose to assume the latter.

"The police want to ask you some questions, Kate." Bradley entered the foyer and must have caught sight of the unconscious wolf passed out at the bottom of the stairs. "Holy shit, is that the…"

"School mascot? Yeah, pretty sure it is. The markings all match up." Seth held up a picture of Bondi on his phone that he'd pulled from Pemberly Brown's website as though other random wolves roamed our town just waiting for the opportunity to attack unsuspecting ex-headmasters.

"What the hell? Why would Sinclair do this? I mean, I know he wasn't exactly in a good place after everything that happened, but this is unreal." Bradley shook his head.

"Right. Well, good luck figuring that out, but do you mind if we squeeze past you real quick? I'd like to get my girlfriend away from the passed-out predator if that's cool."

"I'm not…" I started.

"…Your girlfriend." Bradley finished and held out his hand to me. I looked from Bradley's outstretched hand to Liam's face and stuffed my hands into my pockets. Bradley looked disappointed, and Liam looked triumphant. I did my best to ignore them both.

"Let's just talk to the police. Tell them what's going on…"

"No!" Bradley's voice was sharp. "You know who's in charge now, and believe me, they aren't going to give a crap about some ex-Brotherhood members getting hurt."

Unfortunately, Bradley had a point. Once the Brotherhood had gone under, they lost their foothold not only in our school, but in our entire town. I remembered the moment I'd shown a police detective all of the evidence I'd gathered about Grace's death. I remembered begging him to reopen the case, to put a stop to the societies. But he'd done nothing except to make sure all of the proof I'd gathered was lost forever.

"Look, you guys do whatever you need to do, but I'm not leaving Kate's side until she's back home." Liam looked at me, eyes cold. "I'll call your parents if I have to." His eyebrows flicked in challenge. He knew he had me with my parents. They would not be happy to hear that their daughter was in the middle of yet another crime scene.

"Whatever." I gritted my teeth and tried to ignore the smirk on Liam's face. He'd won this round and he knew it.

"What the hell were you doing in there anyway?" Bradley hissed as we walked back to the family room where the police were waiting.

"Looking for information. And I found it too." I pulled Bradley out the garage door and showed him the card.

"This is a blatant dare. Another freaking dare. What the hell?" Bradley narrowed his eyes at the new clue.

I shrugged my shoulders and took the card back. "Anni. 1964. Page 17. That's got to refer to the PB Anni, right? The yearbook?"

"Yeah, whoever sent this must have something on Sinclair. That was the year he graduated." Bradley shook his head.

The yearbook was a clue, and it was pretty much the only one we had at this point. "Listen, you have to take care of the police, okay?" I nodded back toward the house. "Give them a statement. Get them off our backs. Liam's right. If my parents find out I'm here, I'll be grounded until graduation."

"But I already told them…" Bradley started.

"Well, untell them. You're Bradley-freaking-Farrow."

Bradley smiled a little at that.

"I'm going to go track down that yearbook." I looked over my shoulder at Liam and Seth loitering in front of Sinclair's open garage, doing their best to eavesdrop.

"But it will be archived. You won't be able to get to it unless you know someone on staff."

"Lucky for us, I've got connections." I jerked my head toward Liam.

"Seriously?" Bradley's mouth straightened into a thin line.

"Just manage things here. I'll text you as soon as I find that yearbook page." I squeezed Bradley's hand and turned back toward Liam and Seth, my original knights in shining armor.

But Bradley didn't let go. Instead, he spun me back around, pulling my body into his chest where I seemed to click into place. I lifted my chin in surprise, and before I could even consider how I'd landed in his arms, he kissed me. With Seth and Liam as two of the worst witnesses on the planet, Bradley Farrow's warm lips were claiming my own. My hands were on his chest and I meant to push him away, really I did. But it took me a second too long. I guess maybe there was a part of me that still had a thing for him. The last remnants of first-year Kate who couldn't quite let go of her fantasy boyfriend.

When I finally jerked away, I kept my eyes trained on the ground. It seemed like the only safe place to look at the moment.

"Well." It was the best I could do.

"Some girlfriend," Bradley whispered and walked back into the house.

I really didn't want to turn around and face Liam and Seth, so instead I just barreled out of the garage toward Liam's Jeep parked in the street.

"I need to see an archived edition of Anni," I yelled back toward them while I walked. "It's important, and you're the only one I know on staff." I pulled on the door handle on the passenger side. Locked. Shit.

I finally turned back toward Liam, and he was just a step behind me. A breath away.

He stared at me for what felt like forever. His eyes searched mine, assessing, looking for answers, and then finally he sighed and unlocked his car.

"Fine."

Seth started to climb in the back of the car, but Liam stopped him.

"Kate will get in back."

"But…" I always rode shotgun. Seth always rode in the back. Changing the seating arrangements in Liam's car was like trying to change the law of gravity. Impossible.

"You're not my girlfriend anymore. Remember?" He raised his eyebrow at me, and I wanted to sink into the seat and die right then and there.

"Right." I tried to climb to the back of the car as gracefully as possible under these humiliating circumstances, so naturally the edge of my shirt got caught on the gear shift and I ended up flashing Liam and Seth my gray cotton bra. Icing on the cake.

I heard Seth coughing up front, and I knew he was covering up a laugh. Seth Allen was laughing at me. This was either a whole new low or the end of an era. Probably both.

Chapter 17

A loose thread dangled from the middle seat in the back of Liam's jeep, and I pulled on it to spite him. I imagined the whole car splitting down the middle, falling to pieces. But the Jeep lumbered onward to Pemberly Brown, the backs of Liam and Seth's heads preventing me from indulging in a little backseat driving.

"Red, huh?" Liam asked, raising an eyebrow in the rearview mirror.

I twisted a strand around my finger, flipping it up at the end to check on the color. *Yup. Still red.*

"Uh, yeah. You know what they say," I muttered absently, attacking a split end.

"No, actually, I don't." Liam's voice was clipped. "What do they say?"

Ridiculous stereotypes poured through my brain—blonds have more fun, brunettes are smarter, redheads are bad tempered.

I settled on, "Just that redheads kick ass," and hid my smile. Seth beamed as we all climbed out of the car and headed up the brick path back toward school.

"Subject has connection to Pemberly Brown, Sinclair, the societies, yearbook, the list goes on. It might take a while to locate the appropriate yearbook. Let's not get discouraged." Seth spoke softly and evenly, his head turned a bit to the side as we walked. "Subject should have wolf knowledge—food, habitat, a great love of the animal, and perhaps an unhealthy obsession with Mr. Sinclair." Seth continued speaking, and I noticed he held a Dictaphone that looked like a prop from one of the old-school episodes of *Law & Order* my grandpa watched as reruns.

Liam patted Seth hard on the back, which caused him to stumble on his feet and press pause on the machine. I dropped a step behind, overwhelmed suddenly by how much I missed them. It caught me off guard and took my breath away a little, this hole that I didn't even realize was there. Going to the archives with the two of them just felt right, and my fingers ran the length of the bronze plaque proclaiming, *Scientia est potentia.* Knowledge is power. Wasn't that the truth? I smiled and forgot that Liam and I weren't dating. I forgot that I wasn't supposed to tell Seth anything about the Sisterhood. I forgot that this wasn't supposed to be fun.

The yearbook archives were housed in the stacks in the basement of the Pemberly Brown Library. Despite the fact that books lined the walls and the area was well-lit and, for the most part, not creepy-basement-like, no one really ventured down there alone. Perhaps it was the blue emergency button on the wall or the bookshelves that nearly touched the ceiling and blocked any view between rows that kept girls on their toes, but either way, you told someone if you were going into the stacks and that if you didn't reappear within a few minutes, they should be worried.

"That's 1964, right?" Liam asked, running his fingers over the leather spines.

I referenced the card and nodded my head. "Bradley said it's the year Sinclair graduated. There have to be more clues in there."

Seth continued to mumble into his Dictaphone as Liam typed into the database. I had to work to focus on the screen instead of the way his hair hung over his eye, the way it needed to be cut, the way he shook his head slightly so he could see.

"Aisle 7, second shelf down," Liam said. I rushed to the door, grateful for the distraction.

I turned down Aisle 7 and sent a quick prayer up to Grace. If I'd learned anything about investigating at Pemberly Brown, it was that nothing was easy. Let this be easy, I asked Grace. Let this go quickly.

My fingers ran over the leather-bound books, the gold lettering on the spine. 1961, 1962, 1963, and a space. There was a very obvious hole where Pemberly Brown's 1964 yearbook had been. Despite the fact that Liam suggested we look in other rows for the misplaced book, I knew it had been taken. I knew we were too late.

"Let me just check...it might have been signed out." Liam typed into the database again, referencing the system the staff used to maintain the archives.

And then I remembered the old yearbooks scattered throughout Mr. Sinclair's office.

"Wait, I think I might know where they might be." I made my way out of the maze of books and up the stairs to Sinclair's office. The kid manning the desk protested as I pushed my way into the office. But it didn't matter. When I opened the door, I knew something was very, very wrong.

It was clean. All the papers were stacked neatly on his desk. The stacks of books that had been scattered across the floor had disappeared. The old coffee cups and napkins had all been cleared away. It looked like a normal office. Not a yearbook in sight.

"Unbelievable." My hand flew to my mouth. There was no doubt in my mind that someone had been here. Someone had been looking for something. Maybe the yearbook, maybe something else, but whatever it was, it was gone now.

"Don't see any yearbooks lying around." I hated the quiet note of satisfaction in Liam's voice. Even when he was helping me, it felt like he was silently cheering for me to fail.

"Mrs. ConspiracyLuvR." Seth spoke the name into his Dictaphone and pressed the stop button loudly for dramatic effect. He nodded silently to Liam and me from the doorway of the office. "She's our only hope."

Chapter 18

The nauseating smell of bacon and broken dreams over-whelmed me at the sound of her name. Oh no. No. No.

"Linda graduated in the class of '64. She'll have the book."

"But Seth, you have a rule." ConspiracyLuvR was one of Seth's online buddies who had an extraordinary amount of useless local conspiracy-related knowledge but also a fairly solid understanding of the inner workings of Pemberly Brown. As much as it killed me to admit it, we had depended on someone named ConspiracyLuvR in the past and we would probably have to depend upon him again in the future. The guy's mom? Not so much. Mrs. ConspiracyLuvR was obsessed with Seth, and from what I could recall, it had some-thing to do with his red hair. I shivered as I considered my own newly crimson locks.

"I do have a rule against engaging the Mrs., but what's your rule about breaking rules?" Seth shook his head quickly. "Never mind… you know what I mean. We're going in."

And we were. I only wished I'd brought a gas mask.

ConspiracyLuvR's house was shockingly close to my own. My mom spent way too much time with that sex offender locator tool on the computer, and I couldn't help but wonder why they didn't have some sort of app to identify houses where grown men still lived in their childhood bedrooms. Might come in handy for women screening potential dates on Match.com.

As usual, there were about fifteen beat-down cars parked in the driveway and on the grass. I hoped to God they weren't having some sort of party, couldn't imagine the delays associated with social hour at the LuvR residence. If there was a way to break in and steal the yearbook without getting caught, I would *so* be on board, despite the fact that a stolen yearbook had gotten us into this mess in the first place.

"In and out, guys," Seth whispered. "We get the yearbook as quickly as possible."

He didn't have to tell me.

Movement in one of the cars caught my eye, and despite my better judgment, I peered in. And there, smack dab in the middle of his parents' yard, parked in some god-forsaken car, was none other than ConspiracyLuvR making out with a woman who was clearly in need of the aforementioned boyfriend screening app.

I slapped my hands over my eyes and started screaming. "Ew, ew, ew, ew."

"Jesus!" Liam said, cracking up. "Who the hell are these people?"

He hadn't had the pleasure of a previous visit. We ran the rest of the way up the drive.

The doorbell didn't even have to be pressed. Instead, the door swung open and Mrs. ConspiracyLuvR filled the doorway, permeating the air with her eau de bacon grease.

"I thought that was you!" She spoke in some strange accent—a mixture of faux-British and Southern twang that was probably the result of watching too much reality television. And then she screamed some obscenities in the direction of her lip-locked grown son, who either couldn't hear her or ignored her completely.

Liam widened his eyes at me, his face beet red to stifle his laughter, as Mrs. LuvR yanked Seth into the house. I wasn't sure if I should be thankful or scared that she still concentrated her redhead-loving efforts on Seth. I was a lot of both.

"Just a quick visit, now!" Nervous laugh. "Actually came for a yearbook." Nervous laugh. "No, no. We already ate." Nervous laugh. Poor, poor Seth.

Seth continued to focus Mrs. LuvR on the yearbook and refused four tours of her "renovated" master bath, a couple offers to feed some random parrot named Jimmy that squawked in their family room, and two requests to help load her dishwasher. Finally, she led us into the basement. I hesitated at the top of the stairs. I was 99 percent sure that we were walking into a hoarder's den, and I was afraid that if we descended beneath the ground, we might never come back up. I thought about waiting in the kitchen or, better yet, back in Liam's car, but I couldn't let Seth face this particular wolf on his own. We were in this together. Like old times.

"Y'all excuse the mess, now." Yikes. A mess warning from a woman who reeked of bacon grease was definitely not a good sign. I kept my gaze trained on Mrs. LuvR's yellow muumuu as we wove our way through a maze of junk that included everything from old fax machines to piles of *Playgirl* magazines. She paused for a minute and started digging through a pile of boxes.

"I know it's in here somewhere…" She threw something that looked suspiciously like a dead cat over her shoulder. Seth yelped.

"Ah, yes, here it is. My old memory box. My senior yearbook should be in here somewhere."

I steeled myself for whatever we might find in that box and prayed she'd return upstairs so we could at least have the freedom to make fun of some of it.

"I'll leave you and this young thang to it." Mrs. LuvR pointed a long, acrylic nail in Liam's and my direction. "Seth? How about helping me out upstairs?"

Seth looked from the box to Liam, from the box to me, from the box to Mrs. LuvR, and his face fell as though to say, "I quit." If Seth's loyalty to me and my endless battles could be summed up, it would look a little like the rueful resignation on his face. He patted the box and walked up the stairs with his plus-sized cougar, leaving Liam and me to fight back both laughter and fear for our friend.

We tore through the box with careful precision to avoid things like gray, cotton somethings (we could not bring ourselves to investigate), dried flowers that disintegrated with one touch, chewed pencils, crumpled papers, even a journal, which would have been fascinating to read if we had more time. Finally, at the bottom of the second box, which was full of maternity clothes and yellowed pacifiers, Liam unearthed the old yearbook.

"I need to wash my hands," he said, handing it over with two fingers.

I pulled the card stock from my blazer and flipped to the page scrawled in the message.

A boy cradled a girl in his lap, her cheek resting on his shoulder, smile stretched wide. The boy's brittle smile and flinty gaze made it easy to identify him as ex-Headmaster Sinclair. I pulled the yearbook closer to my face to get a better look at the girl perched on top of him. Her hair spilled over her shoulders in a pin-straight waterfall. She was pretty, but there was something familiar about the way she looked at the camera, hard eyes beneath lowered lashes.

We gasped at the same time, even though we shouldn't have been surprised.

Ms. D.

Chapter 19

Holy sh…" But before I could spit out the rest, my phone buzzed in my pocket.

Taylor.

Headquarters. 6 a.m. Emergency Meeting.

"Shit." I slipped the phone back into my pocket and looked at Liam.

"Yeah, yeah. What happens if you don't show? Will the queen have you beheaded?"

I gritted my teeth. He had no right. "First off, that was a private text. Second off, she's not my queen and you have no idea how any of this even works. If you'd just take a minute and let me…" But I stopped myself right there. I didn't owe Liam an explanation anymore. He didn't get a vote about where I went and what I did. I grabbed the yearbook and made my way toward the stairs.

"I'm trying, Kate. Trying to be your friend. But it's not working. I'm sorry."

I tried to think of a good response, but I came up completely empty. He was trying and I was being a huge bitch. No way around it. No way under it. Only thing I could do was get through it. To figure out who killed Alistair and to end the Sisterhood. Based on this most recent snippet of information, it looked like I might get lucky and end up killing two birds with one stone.

"I'm sorry too." I turned around to look at Liam. I had to say this face to face. "But maybe we're just not meant to be friends right now." *Maybe we're meant to be more. And maybe after I figure all of this crap out, I'll actually be able to give it to you.* I couldn't bring myself to say the words to him because I knew five seconds later I'd be thinking about Bradley-freaking-Farrow and would be more confused than ever. I had some major work to do before I'd be ready to say anything out loud.

We made our way slowly, silently up the stairs, only to find that Mrs. LuvR had Seth cornered in the kitchen and appeared to be trying to feed him some type of quiche. The fact that Seth had his lips pursed and his head turned to the side spoke volumes about his mental state. The word "Victim" should have been written across his forehead like a bull's-eye. Poor guy.

"C'mon, Seth. We've gotta go."

Seth ducked under one of Mrs. LuvR's outstretched arms and sprinted to the front door. "OkThanksForEverythingBye!" By the time I made it outside to the Jeep, Seth was panting in the front seat, buckled in and ready to go.

"Did you get it?"

"Yeah, I've got it right here." I slid into the backseat.

"And?" Seth swiveled around to face me in the backseat.

"And…it's a picture of Sinclair and Ms. D."

"Shut. Up."

Liam threw open the door and started the car without saying a word.

"Now what?" Seth asked.

"Now I go to the Sisterhood and I find out what the hell is going on." I waved my phone in Seth's direction. "They've called an emergency meeting first thing in the morning, and I'd bet my nonexistent trust fund it's about what happened to Alistair and Sinclair."

Liam sped silently to my house. Every shift of the gears felt like an accusation. Seth must have picked up on the tension in the car because he never asked a single question, just did a lot of heavy mouth breathing from the passenger side.

When Liam finally ripped up the parking brake, I scrambled out of the car.

Seth looked worried. "Be careful. We worry, you know."

"I'll be fine. Promise." I took off into the garage. It was only a few yards, but it felt like miles. I wanted to look back at them so badly, but I knew I'd crumble if I did. Seth had this weird way of stripping me down and making me feel vulnerable. He didn't care about looking cool or impressing anyone; he just said whatever he felt. It was unnerving, and unnerving was pretty much the last thing I needed.

And Liam. I'd broken his heart tonight. And mine too. Looking back was pretty much the worst thing I could do for either of us at this point. I reminded myself that there was only one way out of this thing, and that was through. And the more I found out about Alistair and the Sisterhood, the more I realized that this might be something I'd have to get through alone.

Chapter 20

As I peeled my eyes open in the morning, I cursed stupid Taylor and her stupid 6 a.m. emergency meetings with her stupid secret society. Uttering one word to someone before 7 a.m. should be illegal. I couldn't fathom why anyone would intentionally schedule an important meeting where they actually expected people to converse fluently at six in the morning.

A too-hot shower helped a little. Coffee a little more. By the time I made it back to campus, I felt semi-human. I breathed deeply before throwing my weight into the door of the clock tower. My first official Sisterhood meeting lay ahead of me, and I had no idea what to expect.

The old stone walls were covered with pictures of students who had won the prestigious Time Keeper award, and I flipped over prim-looking Veronica Garvey's photograph. She looked a little like pre-makeover Sandy from the movie *Grease*, and I suspected that was one of the reasons Taylor had selected her. After all, Taylor was pretty much the modern-day equivalent in all of her blond, blue-eyed, perpetual-stick-up-her-ass glory. After punching in the code *abscondito*, "secret," a new trapdoor hidden between the planks of the floor popped open and I began my descent into the bowels of Pemberly Brown.

The tunnels have always freaked me out. Ever since learning about the catacombs in Paris in World History when I was a first-year, I could never quite shake the feeling that the walls were lined with the bones of previous Pemberly Brown students. It was impossible not to feel like someone was watching you when you walked down the rickety steps and descended into the dimly lit underground where every footstep echoed and it was at least ten degrees cooler. Not to mention that these tunnels and me? We had a history. And it wasn't really a happy one.

As I turned the corner, I saw the exact spot where Alistair had tackled me and I had stabbed him with one of the swords stolen from the Sisterhood's headquarters. After that, I passed the spot where Liam had been knocked unconscious. And then finally the door to the headquarters where almost six months ago, I had believed I would find my best friend, Grace. Alive and well.

But instead I found Taylor. The Sisterhood. Instead, I found the truth.

And this morning I had to face it all over again. I had to press the buttons on the massive oak door and swing it open and walk back into the belly of the bitch.

Push through. I pressed the code. *Push through.* I held my breath. *Push through.*

The first thing that struck me as the door clicked open was the sheer number of girls in the room. The Sisterhood wasn't huge by any stretch of the imagination. Twenty-one girls total. But having them all in the headquarters at the same time—legs strewn across leather couches, hair streaming over the high backs of antique wood chairs, the high-pitched buzz of excited female voices all talking at the same time—was striking.

For a girl who had spent the better part of her year hanging out with a couple of dudes, it was all a little overwhelming.

Taylor was standing behind a podium, and the instant she saw me walk through the door, she rapped her tiny bejeweled gavel three times. The room went completely silent.

"Now that we are all present…" She shot another pointed look in my direction. I twisted Grace's pearls nervously. "I'd like to call this meeting to order." She lowered her eyes for a second, concentrating, and then lifted her long lashes. "*Una simus,*" she said. "We are together."

"*Una simus,*" we responded at once.

"*Tenemur,*" Taylor continued. "We are bound."

"*Tenemur,*" we repeated.

"*Sumus sorores,*" she finished. "We are sisters."

"*Sumus sorores.*" The words filled every inch of the space, and I let the meaning wash over me. We are sisters.

I am a traitor, I added silently.

"In light of recent events, Headmistress Bower has asked that I clarify our stance on interactions with members of the now-defunct society, the Brotherhood." Taylor took a deep breath and looked around the room, slowly locking eyes with each and every member. "Sisters are not to have any interaction with former members of the Brotherhood. We are unsure of who or what is behind the recent tragedy involving Alistair Reynolds and ex-Headmaster Sinclair, but rest assured the school's administration is working toward a resolution.

"Now that we, the Sisterhood, are the sole surviving society at Pemberly Brown, we have an obligation to our peers and students to keep our school safe, so if you have any information as to who might be involved with this accident, we ask that you report directly to me or the Headmistress. Thank you."

Taylor rapped the gavel again and the girls in the room began to disperse. But not before Naomi's voice rose above all the others.

"Wait," she said, raising a hand and standing. A hush spread over the room, and it became clear that no one usually spoke during these meetings unless they were holding a gavel. Eyebrows raised and eyes widened. "I know Headmistress Bower wants us to stay out of this, but Alistair was my brother's best friend. It's just wrong to ignore it." Naomi lowered her chin and breathed deeply as though she was fighting emotion. "No one wants to talk about Conventus, but can't we work together? Can't we protect each other? Why does it have to be one or the other?"

I couldn't imagine how hard it was for Naomi to say the words, for her to put her own position in the Sisterhood at such risk, but I gave her credit. No one ever questioned these things, barely ever questioned Taylor or the headmistress or anyone in power, and she'd suffer for it.

Taylor opened her mouth to respond, but Bethany walked forward instead, her shoulder pushing Taylor slightly to the side, a bold move. "Naomi, everyone knows where *you* stand. Taylor's explained where *we* stand. Take it or leave it."

A few whispers followed and the room cleared, leaving a stunned Naomi at the center, radical ideas and all. I began to move toward her but was stopped by a strong hand on my shoulder.

"Hey, Kate!" Bethany squeezed my shoulder a little too tightly. "Just wanted to make sure you really understand the meaning of our little meeting. You need to stay away from your little boyfriends, mkay?"

"I'm assuming you mean Liam?"

Bethany's cheeks went pink, and for a second, she actually looked kind of adorable, but half a second later, pink deepened to red and she was back to her terrifying self.

"I mean, boys. Did I stutter? Right now, they're *all* the enemy. So watch yourself, because we'll be watching you." As she turned on her heel, her thick brown hair whipped across my face.

I had the sudden urge to do a fake shiver and say, "Ooh, I'm so scared," like we used to in lower school. But considering the fact that my finger was already tapping a text to Bradley on my way out of the tunnels, I figured I'd give her a break. After all, actions always spoke louder than words.

"And nice try, Naomi." Bethany spun and flashed her teeth. "You saw where Conventus got your brother. Wouldn't want the same thing to happen to you, now would we?"

I half expected her to disappear in a cloud of green, wicked-witch smoke, but she just shot us another syrupy smile and walked away.

Naomi rolled her eyes. "I swear. I don't know why I even bother." I wondered the same thing. "But seriously, ignore her. She's probably just nervous about her big date tonight." Naomi linked her arm through mine.

"Date?"

"Yeah, she finally worked up the nerve to ask out Liam. I thought she cleared it with you first. It's Sisterhood policy." A trace of concern leaked into Naomi's voice.

"Oh, yeah. She did, actually. I'm just kind of…" My mind searched for the words to describe my feelings aside from maniacal anger. "Surprised. I mean surprised that it's so soon. I didn't realize she'd actually gotten around to asking him."

"She texted him last night, and supposedly he seems like he's into it." Naomi informed me in a helpful tone.

"Well, that's just super." I tried to control my sarcasm, but it was hard. Last night, Liam was with me. We had a moment. He tried to talk to me. But I'd shut him down. Again.

So maybe it wasn't exactly surprising that he'd decided to start dating again. Especially after watching me kiss Bradley. But it was shocking that he'd agree to have anything to do with Bethany. She was everything that he hated about Pemberly Brown. And apparently, now she was also his date.

Naomi grabbed my hand and led me through the heavy door back into the tunnels, and I decided that if my life had a soundtrack, it would sound like a super-depressing song from *Les Mis* mixed with the music that accompanied the stabbing scenes in *Friday the 13th*. Too bad I could never seem to find my rhythm.

Chapter 21

It's bad. Come 2 planetarium.

Not exactly a text I was prepared for at 6:26 a.m. Especially not from Bradley when I was walking underground with his sister.

"Crap." I stopped and looked down at my phone. Naomi turned around, concerned. "I forgot my Econ essay at home. I have to go get it before first bell." I turned to head back toward the headquarters. "I'll exit at the gardens. It's closer."

"Oh, okay. I'm sure I'll see you at Open," Naomi said, buying my lie. I just prayed her brother hadn't sent her the same text. "But Kate?"

I stopped walking and turned back toward her.

"You knew about Bethany and Liam, right? The last thing I need is to start something with Bethany." She looked uncomfortable.

"Yeah. Yeah. Of course. It's not a big deal. Liam and I..." I stopped short, having no idea what needed to come next. I waved my hand instead. "I'll see you at Open."

As soon as I heard the hatch shut with Naomi behind it, I rushed back toward the planetarium because it was faster. Huge mistake. It was cold and dark, and I kept expecting to feel someone's clammy hands grab me by the shoulders. I might as well have walked backward, I spent so much time twisting around, but then I worried what was behind me or in front of me or…you get the idea. My footsteps reverberated off the surrounding stone, tricking me into thinking I was being followed, sending shivers up and down my already freezing arms and legs. This better be worth it.

The hatch was heavy as I pushed up and emerged from underground. As my eyes adjusted, I realized the Sisters weren't the only fools to call a predawn meeting. Most ex-members of the Brotherhood stood around the vast room, grimaces stretched across their cocky faces, insults hurtled toward Bradley, who wore the saddest look of all.

"I know you think this is my fault after Conventus, but Dorian's in a coma. We've got to stop this." Bradley's voice shook as the words tumbled out. *Dorian. Dorian. Did he mean Clayton Dorian? Second-year soccer star, green-eyed, blond-haired, sexy surfer-esque Clayton Dorian?* My air supply seemed to have been cut off all of the sudden, and my throat closed. I needed an inhaler or a shot of epinephrine or a new life.

"Dude, you got us shut down," a fourth-year called.

"My brother was suspended," a smaller kid in the back shouted.

After a few more minutes of accusing Bradley of being an

incompetent fool, most of the guys just walked out, leaving a desperate-looking Bradley pacing at the front of the room. Only a couple of kids lingered.

"I heard Granger got a card like Alistair. But he refused to take the bait. And so they went after Dorian," one of them said.

I sat back and did my best to process. Clayton Dorian was in a coma because Michael Granger had refused to perform a Factum Virtus. Whoever was behind this was making good on their threats.

"Please, if any of you get a card, come to me. We'll figure this out together," Bradley was begging.

"Whatever. You're not in charge anymore, Farrow. The Brotherhood is dead." They all started to walk out after that. I waited for the last of the guys to leave before approaching Bradley.

"What now?" Bradley's entire face sagged. His eyes were bloodshot and his complexion waxy. He just shook his head slowly back and forth. I could tell he hadn't nearly begun to grieve the loss of his best friend, let alone digest the fact that another Brother was barely clinging to life. In that moment, I could read his mind. It was easy because there was really only one question left: "Who's next?"

Bradley silently walked out the doors of the planetarium and back toward main campus. Dew scattered across the endless manicured greens of Pemberly Brown like tiny diamonds. I almost expected them to crunch under my toes as I chased behind him.

If the tone permeating the halls of Pemberly Brown was somber before, it veered into dangerously depressing territory after the news about Clayton spread. The counselors had been busy enough after Alistair; now they were inundated. It was clear that something bigger was at play.

I trailed Bradley in the hall as students moved aside to let him through, and I was reminded of the days following Grace's death, after I'd returned to school to find clear paths in the hallway, averted eyes, and whispers following me around like a second shadow. I hadn't missed any of it. And at first, I thought it was happening all over again. I thought they were all looking at me. Whispering about me. I had to assume my new flaming-red hair was whisper worthy. But it was Bradley they tracked. Bradley they whispered about. Bradley's eyes they couldn't quite meet.

My pang of relief felt like a betrayal.

Bradley turned his head slightly but never stopped walking. I could barely keep up. "We raid her office. Tonight. Bring that kid who works there."

"Wait!" I slowed. "Ms. D.'s office?" I whispered her name and stopped in the hallway even though Bradley kept walking. He needed to slow down. He needed to wait for me. He needed to stop. "And Seth?"

He didn't even bother turning around this time. Just nodded his head once and turned the corner, leaving me standing very much alone. Kids filled the path they'd cleared minutes before, and life at Pemberly Brown went on. Because like it or not, that was just how life rolled.

• • •

I climbed into Seth's mom's gigantic white van with its ridiculous stick figure family affixed to the back windshield, featuring a stick mom with an apron (gag), a stick dad with a briefcase (lame), and a stick boy kicking a soccer ball, even though I was 99 percent sure Seth hadn't played soccer a day in his life. They must have been all out of the stick figure geeking out in front of a computer screen. I glanced over at Seth and saw nothing but a shock of red hair and a pale white face. He was covered in some sort of head-to-toe black suit. Footies? I didn't ask.

"Camo," Seth said as he backed down my long driveway. As if I didn't know.

"Comfy," I replied, choking back a laugh. I turned around automatically, muscle memory, looking for Liam, waiting for one of his ever-present one-liners. But his captain seat was empty, and my heart sunk a little. He was probably on his date.

When we made it to Station 1 at the entrance of the school, the closest entry point to Ms. D.'s office via the underground tunnels, Bradley came into view. His perfect features were lit by the glow of the surrounding street lamps, and I let myself forget Liam for the time being. Bradley offered me his hand and I took it. Maybe this was better. Maybe I was supposed to be with someone who was able to understand me and my grief. Maybe Liam was better off with Bethany.

"You know the code, right?" he asked, running his fingers over the bronze plaque fixed to one of the large brick pillars that flanked the school's main doors.

I nodded and counted four (the number of original sisters) bricks over and eight (the number of sisters invited by the original) bricks down from the plaque. I pulled at the loose brick to reveal a small keypad, the bronze keys green with time. Something rustled behind us, and the rhythm of my already pounding heart jumped, thrumming throughout my entire body.

"What was that?" I whispered, jerking my head toward the sound. Seth assumed a ninja-like position against the wall, and Bradley's ears had perked up, his eyes narrowed on the great expanse of black behind us.

We all saw movement at the same time. Two bodies, one slumped against the other.

This was it. The Sisterhood had me. I'd be excommunicated. I was fraternizing with the enemy and I'd be punished.

"Um…help?"

The soft voice was not Taylor's and definitely not Bethany's. It was Maddie's, and when she came into view, she practically carried one very drunk Liam Gilmour. Seth darted over, catlike in his little black suit, and offered a shoulder.

"I'm sorry. I found him in his car and I was afraid he'd drive, and Seth mentioned you'd be here, and I had nowhere else to go. I'm sorry." Maddie pushed a strand of her crazy hair away from her face after she'd been relieved of the Liam lump.

Bradley rolled his eyes. My cheeks were on fire, and Liam smiled, big and sloppy. Perfect, just perfect.

"Guess the big date went well." I tried to look annoyed, but my heart wasn't in it. Better to have him here than out with her. It was selfish and nasty, but that's how I felt. Bradley caught me staring at Liam and laced his fingers through my own. When I yanked my hand away, I told myself it was because we needed to hurry and I was the one who had to punch in the code.

We were going in.

Chapter 22

A door previously hidden in the bricks clicked open a crack, and I pushed through, immediately swallowed by the darkness of the underground.

"What the hell do you think you're doing?" Bradley's voice had dropped an octave, placing him squarely in ass-kicking-bully mode as Liam made a move to follow me down.

"Just following my girlfriend, man." Liam's voice was lazy, practically begging to be punched.

Girlfriend? He had to be kidding, right? Only Liam-freaking-Gilmour would have the nerve to go out on a date with Bethany and then show up here stinking drunk, proclaiming that I was still his girlfriend.

"You sure about that?" Bradley was inches from Liam's face. "Go sleep it off. We don't have time for this."

Liam didn't hesitate before throwing the first punch. Seth started screaming, and I stood frozen. It was like watching someone knock over a glass of milk. I knew something was about to shatter, but I wasn't fast enough to stop it from happening.

Lucky for all of us, Maddie managed to insert herself between Liam and Bradley before Bradley even had time to react.

"Enough. You guys can have your pissing contest somewhere else. But tonight is about Alistair. Or have you forgotten?" She gave Bradley a pointed look.

"And I need Maddie," Seth chimed in. "I mean…she helps at the office too. So she might come in kind of handy or whatever." Even in the darkness, I could see that the tips of his ears were screaming red.

"And we can't leave Liam up here drunk and alone. It's too risky." Maddie grabbed his arm and dragged him down the stairs toward me.

I shot her a grateful smile.

"Well, if you guys are done with this riveting display of testosterone, we should probably get going before someone catches us." I spun on my heel, flicked on my flashlight, and continued walking, not bothering to look behind me to gauge Bradley or Liam's reaction.

It was only a few hundred yards to the stairway that led to Ms. D.'s office. I raced up and pushed on the hatch, grateful to be leading this little mission. Grateful to have something to do aside from dealing with Liam and Bradley. But when I was temporarily blinded by a searing light, I knew something was very, very wrong.

"Well, how nice of you to pay me a visit." Ms. D. sat in her office chair, her snowy white hair closely cropped, not a hair out of place. Her legs were crossed elegantly in the dove-gray pantsuit she had been wearing this afternoon when I saw her after seventh period.

Crap. Crap. Crap. Crap. CRAP.

I sent a prayer up to Grace—or really whoever the hell might be listening—that the others would be smart enough to turn around and go back the way we came. But then Liam's head popped out of the door.

"What up?" He waggled his eyebrows at me and then noticed Ms. D. "Oh…"

"That's quite enough, Mr. Gilmour. Come on in and make room for your friends." She stood and walked toward the door. "Ah, ah, ah, no use running, Mr. Farrow. I see you. You too, Mr. Allen. And Maddie too? I would have expected better of you." She ushered them into her office one by one, her lips pulled back in a straight, thin line.

"Well, now that you're all here, would you mind telling me why you're sneaking into my office after hours?" She sat back down in her chair, her glance flicking over each of us.

I tried to think fast.

"Seth left something in the office and he needed it tonight." The lie flew from my mouth before I had time to think of something better.

"Is that true, Mr. Allen?"

Seth let out a little squeak and nodded quickly.

"Well then, by all means!" Ms. D. waved her arm out. "Please don't let me stop you."

Seth stood up and wobbled like a baby deer who wasn't quite sure where to walk.

"Ok, um, thanks. Yeah, let me just…" He spun around the room aimlessly and finally his eyes lit up a little. "Right! There it is!" He inched toward the lost-and-found box tucked in the corner. "I'm so glad it's here! What a relief!" He held up an unrecognizable piece of fabric with the tips of his fingers and wrapped it around his neck. "My scarf. My Bubby made it for me, and I was so worried about it." He wrapped what looked like a dirty jockstrap around his neck and smiled brightly. "Okay, guess we'll be going."

The rest of us stood up to leave.

"Sit down." Ms. D.'s voice was sharp. Seth shuffled back next to me. Whatever was wrapped around his neck smelled wrong. Just wrong. I stopped breathing through my nose.

"Ms. Lowry." Headmistress D. fixed her bright blue eyes on me. "I trust you will enlighten me, Sister."

I nearly peed in my pants. She was terrifying, and she hadn't wasted any time playing the Sisterhood card, had she? After flying through about a million different alternatives in about half a second, I was forced to do something completely unexpected. I told her the truth.

Ms. D. looked thoughtful and eventually appalled as I showed her all of the evidence we'd collected. From the letters to the article about the headmaster to the yearbook picture of Ms. D., all roads led back to the Sisterhood, which led to the newly appointed headmistress with a major ax to grind against the Brotherhood.

"I see." She pulled her glasses off and snapped the yearbook shut. "Someone is clearly trying to set me up. Or at the very least make the Sisterhood look culpable." She narrowed her eyes toward Bradley, Seth, and Liam. Clearly she did not trust the boys.

"Kate, you have my word that I knew nothing about these attacks against our students. In fact, it pains me to think that you might have considered otherwise."

"But…" I started to ask the obvious question. How the hell were we supposed to trust her?

"I was here tonight laying out an investigation of my own. And it just now occurred to me that we may be of use to each other."

I clenched my hands into fists to keep from biting my nails.

"Kate, I would like you to head up the investigation for me. As a student, you'll be able to access information that I couldn't possibly get to, even as the headmistress. You can infiltrate, my dear!" Oh God, if she only knew. I thought of the Sisterhood. I was already infiltrated up to my eyeballs.

"I don't know…" I started to protest.

"You'll have my full support, of course. And you and your little gang," her eyes moved dismissively toward Maddie and the boys, "will have full access to the tunnels and whatever other resources you might require."

"It's just that…" I tried to figure out the right way to tell her that I'd sooner believe that Seth was wearing Bubby's scarf than that she wasn't somehow involved in this thing.

But she played her trump card before I had the chance.

"I'd hate to have to take disciplinary action against you or your little friends for this unfortunate break-in." She smiled coolly. "After all, you were just trying to help."

If I had balls, she would have had me by them.

"Okay." Even as I uttered the word, I already knew it was a lie. I could still investigate without trusting her. Keeping my enemies close and all that crap.

"Wonderful. I'll expect daily updates. We can meet here after school every afternoon." She stood, which seemed to be our cue to leave. "I'm so pleased this worked out. You and I are going to do great things together, Kate."

But my only response was to step back into the darkness of the tunnels. Two steps forward, five steps back. I felt like I was back in ballroom dancing lessons with Grace as my partner. There weren't enough boys in our gym class so we had to pair up. She was always stepping on my toes and laughing. But tonight, there were no muffled giggles as we made our way back onto campus. Tonight, there was nothing but silence and the sharp sting of defeat.

Chapter 23

By the time Seth dropped me back off at my house, it was past 1 a.m. And worse, both of our houses were blazing with lights. Lit up like freaking Christmas trees.

This was really not my night.

"Well, that's not good." There was a trace of sarcasm in Seth's tone, and I was proud of him for it.

"No, it's really not." I agreed. "Think your parents are going to flip?"

"Nah, my mom always pretends to be mad about this stuff, but secretly I think she's just happy that I have friends." He beamed over at me when he said the last word.

I threw my arms around him. I was just so grateful for Seth and for all he was doing for me.

"What are we going to do?" I mumbled the words into the shoulder of his fleece.

"You'll figure it out, Kate. You always do." Normally I would have made fun of him for sounding like an overenthusiastic preschool teacher, but I was too grateful for the words of encouragement tonight.

"I was so sure it was Sinclair and then Ms. D." I shook my head. "I just can't figure it out, Seth. Why can't I figure this out?"

I was talking about so much more than just who was hurting members of the Brotherhood. I was talking about figuring out who the bad guys were and putting them in jail. It was so easy on the cop shows my dad watched all the time. I just didn't understand why it wasn't working that way in real life.

My parents came running out the front door like a pair of lunatics. I could already hear them yelling something about it being a school night and scheduling an appointment with good old Dr. P. first thing tomorrow morning.

Seth apologized and practically shoved me out of the car. Can't say I blamed him.

"This stops now, Kate. Tonight." My mother's voice was full of anger and fear.

"We love you too much to worry like this, Kate. We're done." My father looked exhausted.

"I'm sorry." It was all I could say, because I couldn't promise them that this wouldn't happen again. I couldn't pretend like I'd had some epiphany that ended with me turning into the person I was before Grace died.

Because no matter how many times I lied to them, how many

times I snuck out or skipped school, I would never stoop to making promises I couldn't keep.

• • •

"So, Kate, your parents tell me there was an incident last night. Care to fill me in?" Dr. P. tapped his fingers together like Hannibal-freaking-Lecter. I wondered if maybe he was a secret sociopathic murderer. Honestly, I might have preferred it that way. At least it would have made our time together a little more interesting.

I shook my head in response. Today I decided to see if I could make it through the entire session without saying a word. It was a huge challenge, but I was feeling pretty good about it.

"Do you think you might be acting out right now because Alistair's death has stirred up some of the same feelings you had when Grace died?" Dr. P. nodded his head slightly and made a little grimace that I suppose was meant to encourage some type of verbal response from me.

I shrugged, drunk on power. Why hadn't I thought of this before? This not-talking thing was amazing. Honestly, it made me wonder why I was talking in general. I bet if I'd stopped talking, I would have finished the Sisterhood off months ago.

"When you act out like this, Kate, you're pushing away all of the people who care about you the most. You're alienating them and alienating yourself."

It occurred to me that Dr. P. was kind of a crappy shrink. I mean, he was literally doing all of the talking and I was just sitting there.

Shouldn't he be pulling some psychiatric kung-fu moves where he matched my silence by not talking to force me to say something, anything? Not that it would have worked, but it would have been kind of awesome if he tried.

"Life is going to continue to throw curveballs, Kate. It's never going to be perfect. You need to learn how to deal with these setbacks head on, but you can't do that until you've finished grieving Grace. You're stuck, Kate. It's common, especially for those who are grieving a very sudden, very tragic loss for the first time."

He paused to scribble something in his notepad.

"The only way out is through."

Those words resonated with me more than I wanted them to. Hadn't I come to the same conclusion?

"And to get through it you need to move past anger, move past this obsession with revenge, and you need to let yourself be sad."

And he lost me. I was so over people shoving me into one stage of grief or another. Did anyone ever really stop being angry after they lost someone they loved? I sincerely doubted it.

My phone buzzed in my pocket and I managed to slide it out while Dr. P. was busy scrawling more riveting tidbits about our session in his little notepad.

The text was from a number I didn't recognize, and there was no message, just a picture.

Liam and Bethany. Kissing. With lots of tongue by the looks of it. He was wearing the same outfit he had on last night, so this little encounter had happened either before or after we got caught by Ms. D.

It felt like someone had dropped a boulder onto my chest. I couldn't breathe. I wanted to cry. How could I have been so stupid? How could I have assumed that he would just be waiting around for me indefinitely? How could I have trusted him? Because when it came down to it, if all of that bullshit about him caring for me and loving me and wanting the best for me had been true, then this picture wouldn't exist.

"Screw it."

I accidentally said the words out loud and Dr. P. jerked his head up in response.

"Yes, Kate, now we're onto something! Screw the grief! Screw the anger! We've made such progress today, a real breakthrough!"

I nodded. Something had been broken all right. Unfortunately, it felt a little bit like my heart.

Chapter 24

My parents kept me home from school, and I turned off my phone and holed up in my room for the rest of the day. I needed time to think.

If Sinclair and Ms. D. had nothing to do with the letters to the Brothers, who was sending them and, more importantly, why? The Brotherhood was over, dead. I couldn't imagine why anyone would go after their former members.

I read the letters sent to each of the victims over and over again. I scanned all of the articles on the headmaster and his half brother. I stared at the yearbook picture of Ms. D. and ex-Headmaster Sinclair. But nothing was adding up, nothing was making sense. Finally I fell into a fitful sleep.

Hours later, I woke with a start. My heart fought my rib cage, knowing before I could that something was wrong. But as my eyes swept across my bedroom, everything was in order. A book hadn't fallen off the shelf. My phone hadn't vibrated across my nightstand,

and neither of my parents was awake. Everything was in place. For some reason, that only made my heart drum faster.

The neighbor's dog barked, and I jolted to a seated position. There was no going back to sleep. I could either crawl into bed with my parents in homage to my seven-year-old self or I could put on my big-girl pants and check things out on my own.

As slowly as I could manage, I untwisted the sheets from around my legs and placed my bare feet on the wood floor. It was kind of an out-of-body experience. I was that girl in the horror movie that everyone in the audience begs not to go down into the basement. Don't turn on the lights. Don't walk outside the tent to explore the creepy noise.

Just. Don't.

And yet I did. And I knew it wasn't going to end well, but I just couldn't seem to stop myself. I made a mental note to quit judging those bimbos quite so harshly in future screenings.

Inhaling deeply, I crept to the side of the window and craned my neck to peer through. The yard was empty, trees still, street clear. A car was parked a few houses down, but the lights were off and the inside completely dark. I let some air escape my lips. Maybe I was imagining things. Maybe I'd just had a weird dream or something.

But then a warm glow lit the side of the house. The neighbor's dog barked again. Someone or something had triggered the motion light in the backyard. It spilled to the front. Someone was out there.

I glanced at my parents' bedroom door shut tight and wondered how alarming it'd be if I threw it open and jumped into their bed. It was their job to protect me, after all. But as I hesitated in front of it, I couldn't bring myself to touch the handle. Besides, if they heard me scream, they'd be out there in two seconds flat. It's not like I was home alone or something.

So my new horror-movie-heroine persona avoided the squeaky steps and tiptoed to the first floor and into the dining room. Long shadows swept across the room from the light spilling in, and I could've sworn they shifted for a split second. Or maybe I blinked. Either way, my hands shook and my knees buckled. Hugging the wall, I inched closer to the window, holding my breath as though it'd give me away. And then the room went black. The backyard was once again doused in darkness, and I could barely see my hand in front of my face. Whoever or whatever had been back there was gone.

As fast as I could, I darted back up to my bedroom, landing heavily on the squeaky steps this time, and jumped into bed. The covers felt like armor, so I pulled them to my chin, my eyes pushed wide with fear.

And there it was.

A single notebook page lay at the center of my room, the loopy orange script visible even in the pitch black. I ran my fingers over the tiny tears that lined the edge of the paper. It looked like someone had just torn it out of her journal moments before leaving it here. In my room. For me.

Grace might as well have been lounging in my bed, pen in hand, cheek resting on her open palm. I saw her as clear as day, could practically hear pen dragging across paper as she wrote her careful words, lips moving silently as her hand slid across the page.

So much for resting in peace.

Chapter 25

From Grace Lee's Journal—September 10

I knew something weird was going on the second I saw the chapel. It was just too quiet or something. According to my little invitation, I was like three days too early, but being fashionably late is for suckers. I needed to know what this place meant and who sent this invitation. I had to know if it was from the Sisterhood.

I googled the crap out of them but only found a couple of mentions. They were some all-girls' secret society that was founded by the same frigid gals that were actually pissed when their all-girls' school went coed. For some reason, the idea of an all-girls' society made me think of girls getting in pillow fights wearing silk camisoles. Ew.

Honestly, I just kind of wanted to know what this whole thing was about. That way, I could just skip it the night of the bonfire if the girls looked like members of the Asian American Club that my parents kept trying to get me to join. The kids in that club weren't even all Asian. They were just all completely lame. I went to one meeting and literally tried to slit my wrists with a plastic ruler. So yeah, if this society *bullshit was just a bunch of National Merit Scholars wearing robes and chanting weird stuff, I was so out.*

But that's not what it was.

First off, there were guys there. Hot guys. Alistair Reynolds and Bradley Farrow. Kate and Maddie would have just about died if they saw them on their hands and knees by the seal. They were looking for something, but lucky for me, all that searching on all fours put them in prime ass-admiration view. I started to move in closer. Purely for research purposes. But then I felt a hand on my back.

I would have screamed, but the girl was too fast for me. She already had her other hand over my mouth. Naomi Farrow. Bradley's sister. I almost ran away from her right then and there. I mean, obviously I shouldn't be there, lurking around. And she was more popular than me, so the ball was firmly in her court. Even worse, she was the best tennis player in our school, so I was pretty sure she was going to take this opportunity to spike that thing in my face.

But that's not what happened. Not at all.

Naomi asked me if I could help her keep a secret. She asked for my help.

And you know what? I'm in. All in. Because this invitation was so much more than I ever could have dreamed of. So much better than I thought. The Asian American Club can suck it, because after the bonfire, we're going to be ruling the whole freaking school.

Chapter 26

It had been precisely four hours and forty-eight minutes since I'd read Grace's most recent words. As I sat beside Bradley after school on his so-soft-it-practically-swallowed-me-whole sectional, I couldn't stop picturing myself tackling his sister, Naomi, and tearing her hair out, chunk by chunk.

Can you keep a secret?

The Naomi in my head asked the same question over and over again. How dare she ask Grace to keep her secrets? How dare she pretend to be my friend?

It hadn't been easy convincing my parents to let me come over here, but in the end a school project and Dr. P.'s urging them to "give me the freedom to overcome my grief" had been enough to get me off lockdown. Bradley rambled on and on about protecting the Brotherhood and figuring out who was behind all of this.

And all I could see was Naomi whispering in Grace's ear. Naomi telling me about the Sisterhood for the first time. Naomi breaking the news about Liam and Bethany. Naomi throwing her arm around her brother.

Naomi.

I'd spent the day as a creeper, narrowing my eyes in her direction, assessing the dark waves that fell down her back and over her sparkling, golden eyes. Why would she do this to me? To Grace? Why lie? Now the only realization that came into crisp focus in my mind was that Naomi was involved in a way she could never admit.

"Right?" Bradley asked, his eyes full of hope.

Crap. I had no clue what the hell he'd even been talking about. "Um…yeah? I mean, yes, yeah!" Wow. Convincing.

Bradley deflated a little, so I blinked my eyes heavily and twisted my body in his direction. It was against pretty much everything I stood for, but I was desperate and I didn't want to hurt him. And I liked the way his hands felt in mine. This at least wasn't a lie. The way his fingers were calloused from holding a lacrosse stick, the surprising softness when his fingers linked with mine wasn't a lie. The energy that flowed up his hand and set my whole body on fire wasn't a lie either.

And then the image of Liam and Bethany making out popped into my head, and I tilted my head back in a silent invitation which he accepted. Greedily. But when his lips came down on mine, I only saw Liam. I only heard Naomi's whispered secrets. When I kissed him, it was a lie.

If only I was in the before-Grace. If I'd been my first-year self, that brown-haired girl with all four years at Pemberly Brown laid out before her like some sort of all-you-can-eat buffet, I'd have surely melted at the first touch of Bradley's soft lips. But the after-Grace Kate knew too much. In the after-Grace, I was kissing him so he wouldn't sense my feelings toward his sister and my complete lack of attention.

God, the after-Grace sucked on so many levels.

Bradley pulled away, concern lining his features. He fell back into the couch, resting his head on a cushion and tilting his chin toward the ceiling. "We'll fix this, right?"

Loaded question. I nodded my head because it's what he wanted me to do.

The silence that bounced between us felt like an opportunity. I jumped on it. "I need to get my phone. My mom read some article about another mom who had a list of cell phone rules for her son, and now she's full of regret and is randomly making up new rules like having my phone charge in their room at night. Um…no." I shook my head, considering whether to continue. "So, I have to, like, check in. You know?" Bradley smiled, and my heart broke a little. He believed me. He believed all of my lies. And it felt like a knife in my chest.

I took the basement steps two at a time and slid into his foyer to get my phone from my book bag. Raising it to my ear, I mocked a call, peeking into the kitchen (no one), family room (empty), and finally standing before the open basement steps so Bradley would hear. "Hey, Mom." I continued talking up the main stairwell, in search of a more private location, namely Naomi's bedroom, to tell my "mom" all about my day.

Please, dear God, let her room be empty.

"We got our tests back in Calc," I said, tapping the door open with my foot. Soft gray walls, splashes of turquoise, dark floors, huge canopied bed, no Naomi.

I had seconds.

"Really well. I studied forever," I continued as I scanned the contents on top of Naomi's desk. An open book, some pens, a calendar, a few papers. Nothing. "Next Wednesday, we'll review for midterms." I rushed to the side of her bed. Phone charger (the Farrows must not have gotten the cell-phone Nazi mom memo). Notebook with mainly blank pages, a few random notes throughout, a thick, black pen tucked inside. *The* pen.

"Not well, she has to retake." I stumbled over the made-up conversation, my voice hushed as I studied the pen. Returning to the book on Naomi's desk, I flipped to her marked page. Her bookmark was a piece of a paper. *The* paper. It was thick and expensive and identical to the paper used in the Brotherhood's Factum Virtutes.

I lowered my phone and snapped a quick picture of the stationery and pen. And then I saw his name. Porter Reynolds. "Study group starts on the sixteenth," I mumbled, running my finger over the script. All day, Bradley had been asking and wondering and worrying about who was going to be targeted by the Brotherhood next.

On the desk, in perfect calligraphy scratched into creamy card stock, was the answer to the question bouncing around in my mind since I'd first laid eyes on the still body of ex-Headmaster Sinclair. It was so obvious, so clear, that I couldn't believe I'd missed it.

Porter Reynolds.

Chapter 27

It wasn't exactly evidence that would stand up in court, but when I thought about it, it made a twisted sort of sense. Naomi with her secret for Grace. Naomi who had just spoken up at our most recent Sisterhood meeting, begging to join forces with the Brotherhood, begging for Conventus. Maybe she thought that hurting members of the Brotherhood would force the societies together. Force the Sisterhood to protect them, force them all to finally become one.

But the pictures from Naomi's room didn't lie. When I brought the evidence to Ms. D., she'd have no choice but to at least consider the possibility that one of her favorite students was an actual murderer.

I expected shouting; I expected the throwing of inanimate objects. I even expected tears.

What I did not expect was this: "Well, pack your bags. You're going to Camp Brown. You'll need a permission slip." She let her voice trail off on the words "permission slip" as if she was already planning my itinerary.

"Um, I'm sorry. I must be missing something here, but I didn't apply for Camp Brown this year. Isn't it too late?"

Camp Brown was a nature preserve located three hours from Pemberly Brown and owned and operated by one of Pemberly Brown's most successful and most eccentric alumni, Siegfried Manchester. He'd purchased the land more than fifteen years ago, and he'd been hosting an outdoor adventure camp and leadership experience every spring break for the past five years. A group of students were selected each year to attend, and supposedly you had to write an essay to apply, but rumor had it that sizable donations to the school carried far more weight than the thousand words punched into a Word doc. Mostly it was a way for rich parents to keep their kids out of trouble while they vacationed in Bali.

"Apply? Of course you did. You're applying now. And congratulations, you've been accepted. Looks like several of your little friends will be in attendance too, most importantly Naomi Farrow and Porter Reynolds." Ms. D. stood up and walked beside me. "My gut tells me she's not involved, but attending the camp will allow you to track her. Can I trust you, Kate?"

Her eyes drilled into mine.

"Yes." I had no idea if I was telling the truth or lying through my teeth. I wasn't even sure that it mattered.

"Good. Then get packed and be at the school by seven a.m. sharp tomorrow. The bus leaves at eight."

I was speechless for the first time in my life. One second, I find out Naomi Farrow might be on some sort of murder spree, and the next, I'm heading to sleepaway camp. Only at Pemberly Brown.

"Keep an eye on her, Kate. Don't let her out of your sight. Porter too. On the off chance you're right about this, we're going to need all the evidence we can get our hands on if we're going to go to bat against the Farrows."

I nodded, already mentally preparing for three days of rope courses, trust circles, and heavy stalking. I started again toward the door, already making lists and plans and excuses for why I would need to stay on top of Naomi like a demented shadow, but Ms. D.'s voice broke my chain of thought once again.

"I believe in you."

My feelings about Ms. D. were complicated. Once upon a time, she'd been one of the people I trusted most in this world, but everything changed when she took her post as headmistress and helped the Sisterhood take over Pemberly Brown. I still wanted to believe that she had my best interests at heart, but it was impossible to trust her completely.

But it was even more impossible to ignore her faith in me. I didn't want to disappoint Ms. D., but I couldn't forget my real goal of destroying the Sisterhood. My best friend deserved it; every girl after her deserved it; and finally *I* deserved it. And maybe gathering evidence on Naomi would help me kill two birds with one stone. Surely the Sisterhood couldn't survive another scandal. Maybe if I proved that Naomi was the one behind Alistair's death, I'd be able to end the societies for good.

Chapter 28

In my dreams, I walked around in super-short shorts, my legs perfectly tanned and toned, wearing a killer pair of hiking boots, while I pummeled Naomi Farrow in front of Bradley and Liam, who were both cheering for me despite the fact that one was her brother and the other pretty much hated me with a passion.

In reality, my skin was roughly the color of ET during his scary, life-threatening Earth illness. My shorts were knee length (camp rules), and my dad, my *dad*, sat next to me on the bus while Bradley was in the way back, plugged into whatever stupid video game he'd packed for the long bus ride.

Needless to say, the sure-you-can-hop-away-on-an-extended-camping-trip conversation I'd planned on having with my parents didn't exactly pan out. Even after a very convincing episode of heart-wrenching sobs and swearing that they were ruining my life, my dad said the only way I would be bussing it to Camp Brown was if he was with me. As a chaperone.

He was currently involved in a very animated discussion about the future of car travel with my Econ teacher across the aisle.

I had visions of the bus careening off the road into a ditch and exploding into flames. At least I wouldn't have to hear about how cars would eventually drive themselves on freeway rails while running on a combination of human waste and vodka.

While my dad waxed poetic about the safety of poop mobiles on my left, Seth was fast asleep in the seat on my right. He made a series of slapping, licking, tasting, most disgusting tongue sounds on the planet, and I elbowed him sharply in the ribs.

"What? Maddie? Sunset? Campfire?" He rubbed the sleep away from his eyes with the back of his hand and flushed. "Oh…Kate. Sorry. Was I talking in my sleep?"

"Yeah totally. Something about a very intimate moment between you, Superman, and Wonder Woman." I managed to keep a straight face while his cheeks were about burst into flame.

"Well, it's totally normal for guys my age to have fantasies…"

"Oh God, no. Stop, just stop. I was kidding."

"Works every time." It was Seth's turn to laugh.

"Well played." I tipped my imaginary hat to him and lowered my voice to a whisper. "Actually, I was just wondering if you had a chance to talk to Liam. About the plan?"

Seth's green eyes flicked to the back of the bus where Liam sat between Bethany and Naomi. Every so often, we could hear the three of them laughing. The sound made me want to kill someone.

Liam hadn't so much as looked at me since the night we'd all landed ourselves in Ms. D.'s office.

Seth patted the back of my hand. "You know, it's okay to be jealous, Kate." He popped a Raisinet in his mouth, which reminded me way too much of those cars my dad was still rambling on about. "I've been there, believe me."

"I am not jealous, okay? I'm just tired. And stressed. Excuse me for wanting to make sure that no one else gets hurt."

"But it really seems like…." I gave Seth the look of death (patent pending), and he stopped mid-sentence. "Uh yeah, Liam's on board," he finished.

Because of the most recent Naomi twist, Bradley had to be completely snipped out of the investigation without knowing about said snipping. It hadn't been easy. Luckily (or really, unluckily), Bradley was still distracted by grief for Alistair. I pushed up on my seat with my hands to peer down the aisle and saw the top of his shaved head. Even that looked pissed off. It was cocked to the left and lowered slightly. He'd resisted the trip but had come at his parents' and teachers' and counselors' insistence to escape and relax, but mainly to heal. Or so they promised. I had my doubts.

• • •

Camp Brown met us with the fresh smell of a forest in bloom and blinding sun we had to squint our way through. I sneezed seven times in a row. An auspicious beginning to our little adventure.

A guide named Luca instructed us to strap on our backpacks

and prepare for the hike to camp. Siegfried Manchester, inventor of Bye Bye Diaper, a contraption that somehow reduced the size and smell of a dirty diaper into an environmentally friendly nugget, had created the adventure camp as a way of giving back to his alma mater. Every year, students were selected to be bussed out here, placed on teams, and forced to compete in team-building challenges designed to shape future leaders of America, followed by a mandatory three hours of Reflectere to set personal goals and review accomplishments. It was Pemberly Brown meets *Survivor*, but with bug spray, secret missions, and rum smuggled in shampoo bottles.

"It's so pretty out here." I wrapped my arm around Bradley's waist as he gazed at the lush, green-covered hills in the distance. The trees stretched for miles, and it felt like we were on a different continent, as opposed to just three hours from school. As birds chirped and the brand-new spring leaves rustled in the wind, it struck me how isolated tragedy could be. While Pemberly Brown seemed to be crumbling between our fingers, the rest of the world was welcoming spring. It was unfair and comforting at the same time.

Bradley nodded and squeezed my hand. I knew how hard he was trying, and despite everything I'd been through with Grace, I couldn't imagine how he was feeling right at that moment. I couldn't bring myself back to that place. I wouldn't let myself think about how much we were deceiving Bradley by investigating his sister. It was unforgivable. As unforgivable as Naomi's involvement in the first place.

Once again, I found myself wedged into a tight corner, damned if you do, damned if you don't, and all that. For once, I wished I didn't have to use anyone. I wished something could be easy. I wished that I wasn't always stuck being the Trojan horse.

Liam laughed with Naomi and Bethany a few yards away. He was already at work, cozying up to Naomi. I couldn't stop the stab of jealousy as I watched him throw his arm around her shoulder. Even worse was the look on Bethany's face as she watched them. She so clearly had a thing for Liam, and based on the picture someone had so helpfully texted me the other night, the feeling was mutual.

Bradley, I reminded myself. Focus on Bradley. Focus on the plan. Focus on the Sisterhood. All this crap with Liam could wait, and even if it couldn't, he'd clearly already moved on. What was stopping me?

"Maybe we can hike up there or something," Bradley said, nodding to the great expanse of green. I let my eyes linger for another second on Liam's dimpled smile and turned back to Bradley, to his sad but hopeful eyes.

"Definitely," I said, squeezing his hand back. "I'd love to."

And then a voice seemed to erupt from the trees. It came from nowhere and everywhere all at the same time.

"Ladies and gentlemen, welcome to the seventh annual Survivor Games!"

Chapter 29

Horns erupted, fireworks exploded. I saw Seth fall flat to his stomach and shimmy to the nearest copse of trees for cover.

"Wait? What? They fight to the death? Oh, no. That's not what I intended. Not at all. Well, shoot…" The voice was still on the loudspeaker but sounded decidedly less grandiose. All of the students stood looking at each other, trying to figure out if this was some kind of joke.

There was a strange shuffling noise over the speakers and then finally, "I mean welcome to the seventh annual Pemberlympics!" More fireworks exploded. Classical music blared from the speakers.

A tall, gangly man in a full suit and bow tie burst from the trees with a small microphone in his hand.

"I'm your host! Siegfried Manchester!"

The man only spoke in exclamation points. There was a smattering of applause as he took a bow, revealing his sweat-soaked back to his small audience of students and chaperones.

"Welcome to Camp Brown! You have been carefully selected to compete in a series of mental and physical challenges over the next few days! The winner will receive an internship with my company this summer!"

"Whoa, watch out. I'm going to kick your ass for that internship." Bradley's voice was laced with sarcasm. Poor Siegfried gave away an internship every year as the grand prize for his weird competition, having absolutely no idea that students actively tried *not* to win it. No one wanted to work over the summer, and most of the kids were forced into this trip by their parents. So the competition actually involved performing the worst without getting caught actively losing.

So, yeah, I was pretty much born to win this game. Er…lose this game? Whatever. There was no way in hell I was getting stuck with that internship.

"As tradition dictates, you will be living in cabins! One with nature! And our first competition will decide your roommates and partners for the remainder of your stay!"

I caught Liam's eye. But he just looked away and threw his arm over Naomi's shoulders.

"There are backpacks hidden in the woods behind me. You will be grouped in rooms by color with one chaperone per cabin. The person who finds the golden pack will stay with me in the executive cabin and wins the first challenge!"

Right. So it was basically a game of hot potato in the middle of a forest. Whoever got stuck with the golden pack was totally screwed.

Seth started sprinting toward the woods, fierce determination written across his features. Siegfried pulled a small starting pistol from his pocket and shot a blank into the air.

"Freeze, Ginger! The games have yet to begin!"

I busted out laughing. I couldn't help it. This whole thing was just too awesomely ridiculous for words. To my surprise, Bradley started laughing too. Then Taylor and Bethany. And Maddie. And Liam. And finally, even Seth and Naomi. It was the kind of laughter where you knew it was going to get you in trouble, but that just made the whole thing even funnier. Even my dad and my Econ teacher were doing some suspicious coughing that made me pretty sure they were choking back giggles.

"Now! Now! Order! I mean…" Siegfried shifted uncomfortably from foot to foot like he had to pee. "Let the games begin!" He fired more blanks into the air, and this time everyone took off.

Naomi and Liam darted to the left and I followed them, keeping a slower pace. I had to see Naomi's color bag so we could be in the same cabin, but I quickly lost sight of them in the dense woods. Crap, crap, crap. There was no way I'd be able to keep an eye on her if we were separated. I saw a bag in the trees and made a grab for it. I could always hold on to it until I found Naomi again and then ditch it somewhere if she had a different color.

I pulled the straps over my shoulders and kept running.

"Naomi, take this *red* one!" Liam's voice rang out in the woods.

I sent him a mental thanks and started on faster, desperate to find another red bag. All around me I heard shouts of joy and a few curses. Slowly but surely, all of the packs were being taken, and I still hadn't found a red one. I was running out of time. Shit, shit, shit.

And then the gunshots rang out again. More music followed by Siegfried's voice. "All of the packs have been located. Report to camp for your assignments and for the winner announcement."

I made my way out of the shade of the trees and onto the beach next to the lake where the rest of the students had already gathered. I scoured my fellow campers, searching for red. I found Naomi first, triumphant and cradling her red bag like a baby. Bethany and Taylor were wearing matching blue packs. Maddie and Seth had blue too. Now that was going to be an interesting room. Yikes. Another shot of red, this time Porter Reynolds. Oh God, please let Liam have the last red, please, please, please.

I felt a tap on my shoulder and I turned around to find Liam, eyebrow cocked, red backpack at his feet.

"I'm impressed." I was actually more grateful than impressed, but he didn't need to know that.

"No, I'm the one who's impressed."

"What do you mean?" Was he trying to be a dick? Yeah, I hadn't gotten a red, but at least I had yellow. It was better than getting stuck with our weird-ass host.

"I mean, you got the gold! Congratulations!" Liam slapped me on the back.

"Very funny. It's yellow, you…"

But I didn't have time to finish my sentence because Siegfried was already moving toward me like a bow-tie-rocking missile.

"Our winner! Our winner! Congratulations, young lady! You are now in first place!"

"Yellow." It was the only word that came to my lips, and as soon as I said it, I knew my mistake.

"Oh no, it's gold! You got the gold!" Siegfried took my arm and swung me into what could only be described as a victory jig.

Apparently, I wasn't very good at losing.

Chapter 30

I tried to imagine a scenario where a Pemberly Brown student would actually try to win the first challenge because the way I saw it, I had just landed in my own personal version of hell. The cabin was spacious and had absolutely no characteristics of an actual cabin (thank God). The marble bidet was only trumped by the constant questions from my dad about how I was feeling and the awkward staring from Siegfried. It was like being under house arrest, only instead of a DUI and an ankle bracelet, I had a slightly suspect mental history and a yellow backpack.

"Young lady," Siegfried said for the millionth time. I'm not sure if he really couldn't remember my name or if he was trying to make me uncomfortable. If I was a betting woman, I'd probably say both. "You are in a very good position. Very good. Throughout your stay in this cabin, I will give you tips and advice to secure your standing as number one."

My dad raised his eyebrows at me and smirked. I scratched my eye using my middle finger and shot him a meaningful look, a move that probably would have gotten me grounded at home, but my dad just laughed. Turns out Camp Dad had a decent sense of humor.

"You also have the opportunity to spend your daily free time with me as your mentor."

"Oh…um…wow. Neat." "Neat" was about two steps removed from "groovy" when it came to outdated jargon. What the hell was happening to me? I had to get out of there. "It's just that, Ms. D., our headmistress, she made it a point to remind me to spend time with my classmates. Especially during free time. You know, to build relationships?"

I backed toward the door, clutching my bathing suit and towel as though I was inching away from a pack of wild animals. Every chaperone appeared amused except for Siegfried. He looked hurt, but not hurt enough to guilt me into hanging around. My butt hit the swinging door and I pulled a Seth, sprinting as fast as I could across the grounds to the red team's cabin.

The thump of bass pumped through every crack in the cabin, out cracked windows, and beneath the door. The red team's chaperone, some bored-looking housewife, sat outside on a step texting on her phone. It was worlds away from Casa Siegfried across the way, the full-fat caramel macchiato to my stale police-station coffee.

Housewife shifted on her butt to make room for me to walk up the steps and offered a sympathetic smile at my sorry state of affairs over in the golden cabin. Before I could even open the door, Naomi came spilling out laughing and grabbed my arm to yank me in.

"Kate!" she screamed, her golden skin shimmering beneath a gauzy cover-up. The entire space smelled like coconuts and fun. "We were just going to come and find you. We're going in the lake!"

I wanted to love her for thinking of me, for her bubbly personality and the magnetism that radiated off her in waves. You couldn't *not* like Naomi Farrow. It was an impossibility. But then I caught sight of Liam, his eyes locked on Porter who was splayed out on his bunk, face turned toward the wall. Alistair had been caught in the crossfire just like Grace. Porter had lost a brother, Bradley a friend, and all for nothing. Alistair's death didn't stop anything. It wasn't a call to arms, didn't spur a new set of rules. It was a domino effect. Clayton Dorian was still in the hospital.

Anyone could be next. And Naomi Farrow was the problem, not the solution. We were like two poles on the same magnet, pushing against each other without even knowing it. Or maybe I was wrong. Maybe she knew exactly what she was doing.

"The dressing room's open. Go change!" she said, her white teeth flashing in the sun that streamed through the open windows. I held on to her eyes a bit longer than normal, wishing I would see something there, some glimmer of truth, but she flushed and looked down before anything became clear.

"Right. I'll just be a second." As I adjusted my bikini behind the closed door, I gazed at the lake sparkling under the late-afternoon sun. Even though it was unseasonably warm for April, the water would still be frigid. But no Ohio girl would ever pass up an opportunity to get some sun on an actual beach. This should have been fun. My biggest concern should have been figuring out how to convincingly lose Siegfried's lame challenges. But the beach, the forest, the charming cabins were all laced with a bitterness that burned my throat and left my stomach raw.

A sense of foreboding gurgled and twisted inside, and even the sight of the pebbled sand and the surprisingly blue lake water couldn't calm me. Laughter erupted behind the closed door, and I realized my time was up. I'd just have to shadow Naomi as we'd planned, and maybe everything would be okay.

All of us trekked to the beach, even Porter and Bradley. I couldn't help but notice the circles that ringed Bradley's eyes. Having Porter around was hard on him, a constant reminder, but his smile shook less than it had in days, and he was laughing his real laugh, so maybe things were getting easier. Maybe this trip really was helping him work through some of his grief.

Maybe it was helping all of us.

"We're lucky, you know?" Naomi cradled her head in her hand and turned on her towel toward me. "Pemberly Brown can be totally messed up sometimes and I hate that my brother is hurting and that you…" she hesitated. "Well…you know, but we're still lucky. I mean, we're *here*."

Maddie squealed as Seth splashed her with the cold water, and Liam played Frisbee with a bunch of the guys. Bradley had passed out a few towels down, and the beach was dotted with students and chaperones. Bethany and Taylor gossiped quietly on a beach blanket. Even Siegfried had come to play. (He'd left his bow tie at the hut.)

I wanted to believe that Naomi was right. That it was luck that we'd been selected for this trip. Luck that we were here while our friends were dead and buried. Luck that I had been the one to lose a best friend, the one whose life was divided forever by death.

But there was nothing lucky about it.

I re-tied my straps and propped myself up on bent arms. "Sometimes I think we make our own luck. Or someone makes it for us."

I waited to see if Naomi would bite, but her eyes remained trained on the water. We sat there in silence, watching the birds swoop overhead. Later, we shrugged back into our cover-ups and began preparations for the nightly bonfire.

Siegfried and the chaperones spoke vaguely about the morning challenge and our responsibilities to set goals. Because of my golden pack status, I led the three parts of Reflectere—*Venimus*, "We have come;" *Lusimus*, "We have played;" and *Vicimus*, "We have won."

The fire died down to a sputter and someone yawned, setting off a yawn chain around the circle. If we wanted to perform well tomorrow, Siegfried suggested we sleep. In that case, I wondered if I should pull an all-nighter.

"Are we cool?" Liam asked, elbowing me lightly.

I had no idea how to respond to that question. He'd barely said two words to me over the past few days. I'd seen actual photographic evidence of him making out with Bethany, and he was currently spending all of his free time with another girl in hopes of catching her doing something shady. There was absolutely nothing cool about any of it. And yet, what could I really say? I was the one who told him we were over. I was the one who kissed Bradley. I was the reason he was spending all of this time with Naomi. This was all my fault.

"Yeah. We're cool." I glanced behind me and lowered my voice. "You'll watch her, right?"

"I'm on it," he replied, rolling up his towel.

Liam. He had resisted and fought me and pushed any involvement away, and now, as he walked back to the cabin only a beat behind Naomi, I wondered what had changed his mind. It couldn't have had anything to do with me. But that didn't stop a flicker of hope from melting just a little of the ice that surrounded my heart like a cage.

Chapter 31

What could only be described as a mind-numbingly loud siren ripped across the rolling hills of Camp Brown, and as it yanked me from sleep, I knew instantly that someone had died, a tornado was coming, or the zombie apocalypse had begun. Possibly all three at the same time.

I slapped my hands over my ears, my eyes still blurry with sleep. But instead of crying, hunkering, or defending one's self against flesh-eating non-humans, all the chaperones in my cabin were laughing. At me.

"Good morning, sunshine," my dad quipped. I fell back onto my pillow with a groan.

"Up, up, up, number one! We have a challenge to win!" Siegfried fluttered around the room like a butterfly on speed. I seriously considered suffocating myself under the pillow.

By the time every camper had dragged their body from the cabins dotting the lawn, eyes still bloodshot from the most unnatural wakeup call of our lives, I was afraid we all might start turning on each other like savages. Even Naomi, perpetually supermodel chic, appeared tired, mussed, disgruntled.

"Coffee," we mumbled in unison. No matter how many times we were told coffee would stunt our growth, at Pemberly Brown, we were accustomed to our daily Starbucks runs and the caffeine jolt that followed. Starting the day with anything less was torture. Especially when we were ripped from sleep by a freaking siren. And like a mirage waving in the distance in the Sahara Desert, large canisters of coffee came into view, situated along the perimeter of Centrum, the centermost point of camp. We stampeded to claim our cup, and after each of us warmed our hands around the liquid gold, all was right in the world.

Camp Brown spread out from Centrum, a center point designed by Siegfried himself. He'd placed the first brick, rumored to be borrowed from one of Brown's old school buildings. The rest of the smooth rocks swirled out from that point creating a rustic, circular mosaic and the perfect meeting spot. Siegfried stood on that first brick, megaphone in hand despite the fact that we could have heard him whisper.

"Girls and boys!" Siegfried spoke into the megaphone, and we slapped our hands over our ears again. Taking the hint, he lowered the contraption. "Welcome to the second challenge, *Merge aut Nata*," Siegfried explained. He wore a gold T-shirt and winked at me. A few kids laughed and my cheeks caught fire. *Sink or swim*, I thought, translating the Latin. Kind of summed up my life right about now. He lifted up a pile of gold T-shirts.

"The winners of today's challenge will receive these." "Victor" was printed across the chest of five T-shirts. "They will also have the opportunity to join me in Chicago this summer at my company's headquarters. Unlike years past, this summer's internship will employ a group of Pemberly Brown students." A few kids raised their eyebrows. Sure, no one wanted to work over the summer, but Chicago changed things a bit. Cute apartments came to mind, the lake, boutiques. An internship at Bye Bye Diaper suddenly wasn't sounding so bad.

Chaperones began circulating, handing each of us a small ticket. We all opened our tickets, and whispers increased in volume as kids began comparing and even trading. My Econ teacher raised one arm in the air.

"All right, all right. Listen up. Your ticket designates your team for this challenge. We'll organize ourselves by color, and uniforms will be distributed." He indicated positions for team members to gather, and in seconds, we'd arranged ourselves into teams.

Sure enough, Naomi sidled to my side and elbowed me playfully. "I'm gonna keep my distance, number one," she joked. "I'm staying local this summer."

I laughed awkwardly with my stomach clenched. How could Naomi do that? How could she go from suspect to friend in seconds? Why did she have to make everything so confusing?

My Econ teacher handed me a bright green wetsuit I was to wear during the challenge. Taylor was handed green as well. She raised her eyebrows at me in understanding or solidarity or judgment. I couldn't be sure which. As I unfolded the material, I noticed white lettering positioned across the front. *Conventus.* "To come together. To join. To unite."

The word took my breath away like some sort of epiphany. Naomi carefully unfolded her suit and ran her slender fingers over the letters. Her eyes flashed to her brother's a few groups over. Naomi and Bradley stood for a union of the Sisterhood and the Brotherhood. Their dream, their parents' dream, was for the societies to merge so power would be distributed evenly. If I hadn't been completely manipulated by Taylor and Bethany, they might have actually succeeded. And yet, I couldn't help but wonder what our school might look like if they had. Would Alistair be alive? What about Clayton? Would the Factum Virtus have even been resurrected?

I couldn't be sure about anything anymore. My eyes flashed back to Naomi, who raised her eyebrows at her brother. In that moment, I wondered just how far two people might go to accomplish a family dream. Would they set the Brotherhood up against themselves to prove a union was necessary? Would they trick? Would they kill?

I touched each letter of the word the way Naomi had just seconds before. "Conventus," I whispered, loud enough for Naomi to hear. She turned from her brother to me.

"Conventus," she replied.

Chapter 32

As soon as we'd all suited up, we traveled in pods of color to the lake. Situated in four piles along the edge were an inflatable raft, two oars, and a length of rope.

"Each team has a lane," our Econ teacher shouted. My dad arranged colored posters in front of the lane lines bobbing in the lake. "When the start gun is fired, you will work together to inflate the raft, situate every team member on the raft at the same time using the rope to stabilize yourselves, and use the two oars to row the length of the lake. If a team member falls into the water, your team's time will be restarted. You must have every team member balanced on the raft to clear this challenge. Once your team has reached dry land, you must deflate the raft and zip it back into its bag." He raised an impossibly small nylon bag in the air. "The team with the lowest time wins." He smiled and rubbed his jaw. "Good luck."

Seth beamed in his purple wet suit. There was nothing he liked more than a good team-building activity, and I knew he'd give anything to join Siegfried in Chicago this summer. The rest of his team looked a little bored, rounded out by Porter, who looked shattered. A spattering of members on other teams looked excited at the prospect of a summer in Chicago, which would make the challenge particularly interesting as some would try to lose and others win. Not to mention the fact that the challenge was borderline impossible. There were five people on each team. Five people plus a cheap raft meant for one seemed lofty at best.

But we had to win. I was beginning to think that the farther Naomi and Bradley were from Pemberly Brown this summer, the better. I'd worry about myself later. I surveyed my team. Taylor held hands with Bethany and jumped up and down excitedly. They seemed like they were in it to win it in spite of the fact that Bethany was half giant and might be difficult to balance on the raft. Naomi strategized with Bradley.

"Teams get ready!" Siegfried shouted, pointing a small start gun into the air. Smiles spread around the crowd in anticipation of the crazy challenge, and everyone huddled around the supplies. "And go!" One shot was fired, and rafts were yanked from the bag. Apparently a team trip to Chicago was too much to pass up, because everyone worked fast.

Taylor took position in front of the raft as the first person to inflate it while Bethany and I smoothed the wrinkles. Naomi held a corner and Bradley raised his eyebrows. When Taylor grew tired, we switched and began to make headway, the raft slowly coming to life. Seth's purple team circled around an almost-inflated raft, strategizing before throwing it into the lake. This would be close. Blue wasn't far behind. Liam's orange team was a hot mess of laughter and arguments.

The real fun came when we all tried to pile on the raft. Bethany was the first to board, using the oar against the edge of the beach to stabilize herself. Barely. Taylor came next, the raft tilting at precarious angles. When Bradley loaded, the entire thing capsized from the center out, restarting our team's clock. Taylor pulled herself from the water in her typical dramatic fashion, and I found myself biting back laughter. Other teams were giggling and shouting at soaked teammates.

"We need a better plan," Naomi insisted, pointing to the letters on her suit. "We have to work together."

I narrowed my eyes. This coming from the girl willing to do just about anything to fulfill her family's dream. Even murder. Bradley pouted near shore, water up to his torso, droplets glistening off his shaved head. He didn't lose well. Taylor wrung out her hair and nodded in agreement.

"Bradley, you need to load first. You're the heaviest," Naomi informed him. "But stay low to the raft. Let's squeeze as close together as possible. If we run out of space, Kate, you can sandwich on top of Bradley. You don't mind, right?" She laughed in my direction, her eyes sparkling.

"Of course not," I said, keeping my voice steady. And yet…

Bradley jumped on the raft belly down. Bethany loaded next, grabbing the rope Bradley held out so she wouldn't tip. She squeezed in as close as she could so Naomi could fit on the other side. The raft wobbled, but didn't flip with Naomi's weight. Taylor clung half on, half off as the raft threatened to tip, but finally jumped into the pile as everyone clung to the edges. I held my breath and everyone, soaking wet around me, did the same. Water splashed over the side, but she made it, the raft stabilizing after a few seconds. I could tell the raft was full to capacity, that my weight would surely tip the entire thing. It probably wasn't worth even trying. But Seth's team in the last lane was just about as close as we were. I couldn't let them win.

Instead, I geared up and slid my body on top of the pile. Bradley tensed as I positioned myself, the raft tipping to the left and then the right and almost buckling in the middle. The orange team cheered, having all but quit the challenge. Seth's team was halfway across the lake, teetering but rowing.

"Come on, guys!" Naomi cheered from her position. "Conventus!" She just couldn't help herself.

The word was distracting to me, the raft swaying dangerously beneath us. I glanced at our competition, square in the center of the lake, attempting to reach one of the oars that had fallen off the side. We were still in this. My fingers wrapped around the oar and I pulled it in, using a lane marker to stabilize myself as best as I could.

I pushed the oar into the water and got the raft moving. Soon we were positioned close to Seth's team, one ridiculous pile of people neck and neck with another. And then the second I thought we had the win, the moment I pictured Naomi and Bradley miles away for the summer, removed from the equation, we were under the water instead of on top of it, the raft flinging out from under our weight.

"Congratulations, Purple Team, and congratulations, Ms. Lowry!" My flaming hair was plastered to the sides of my face and I choked on lake water when I heard Siegfried say my name. "You have all won internships with my company this summer!"

"But I lost!" I sounded like a petulant child, but I was too cold and too tired to care. A summer internship sounded like the most miserable form of punishment. Especially if it meant leaving Naomi and Bradley behind.

"You won the first challenge, Ms. Lowry. That has not gone unnoticed." Siegfried's eyes were kind, and my dad gave me a double thumbs-up from behind his back. Of course he wanted me away for the summer. He probably thought getting away from Pemberly Brown might help me heal or at least help me forget.

Yeah, right.

And the cherry on top of my melting glob of ice cream was when my eyes landed on Liam on the beach beside Bethany. She had him wrapped in her arms and was whispering something into his ear. Suddenly being hundreds of miles away from my life didn't sound so terrible.

Chapter 33

The sky had turned the kind of inky black that only exists outside of the city. The night was so clear that I felt like if I just stretched high enough, I might be able to reach up and pluck out one of the millions of stars sparkling in the sky.

Siegfried had pulled out all of the stops for our last night. The rich smell of charred pig laid out on a spit had the boys salivating and the girls gagging, but the tables heavy with wood-grilled pizzas, fresh fruit salads, and an array of bite-sized desserts meant that there was something for everyone.

Well, everyone except me. I didn't have much of an appetite when I considered heading back to Pemberly Brown, back to Headmistress Bower, having made absolutely zero headway with anything. For all I knew, another Factum Virtus had been delivered and some ex-Brother was in serious danger. Bradley's expression was blank, his eyes fixed on the great lake spread out before us, seemingly unseeing. And then there was Porter, equally vacant, as though he were glued back together without any of the pieces fitting together in the right way. I had nothing.

I had to go.

And I had no one to tell. I made my way over to the food tent. My dad had a full plate of food. I moved past the buffet line and found Bethany and Naomi laughing with Liam. Seth. I had to find Seth. Searching the crowd, I finally spotted his red hair a few yards down on the beach. He would care that I was calling it a night, that I felt defeated in every way possible. He'd walk me back to my cabin and promise me that everything would be okay.

But when I started toward him, I noticed that his head was tilted kind of funny. And then I saw another curly head of hair. Brown frizz attached to Maddie's face. Maddie's head close to Seth's. Their lips touching. Oh my God, my best friend was making out with my ex-best friend. It felt like watching siblings stick their tongues down each other's throats.

Oh God, oh God, oh God. Why was this happening right now? The only two people I could really talk to were engaged in the grossest make-out session of all time, and I wanted to scream.

So I ran. I ran because that was what you did when you found your best friend making out with your other best friend and it brought up even more confusing feelings that you had absolutely no idea what to do with and you'd managed to fail at the one thing that gave you even the slightest semblance of control and you had absolutely no one to talk to about any of it.

But as I sprinted past Naomi's cabin, I stopped and noticed the door was ajar. I looked back toward the party and saw Bradley sitting stone-faced in front of the fire. Instead of really thinking about what I was doing, I let my body move instinctively. I slipped into the cabin.

If I could just find some evidence, something to prove that she had hurt Porter, then maybe this night wouldn't be a waste after all.

It didn't take me long to locate Naomi's huge duffel. It smelled like gardenias and expensive leather. It smelled exactly like what every perfume ever bottled aspired to smell like. It smelled like hot girl.

Within thirty seconds, I had the contents of her bag laid out across Bradley's bed. My hands pressed against the thick satin lining, feeling for something hidden there. Maybe a Factum Virtus, paper, the pen, anything. There had to be something. There was no way her bag was really just full of bathing suits and overpriced grooming products.

"Find what you're looking for?" Like his sister's perfume, Bradley's voice was overprivileged and kind of unmistakable.

"Nope." I decided it couldn't hurt to be honest.

"What the hell are you doing, Kate?" He was standing next to me in two big steps and stuffing Naomi's belongings back into her bag. "One second you're all over me, the next you're in here alone digging through my sister's stuff." Without warning, he closed the remaining inches between us, and his eyes ground into mine, his body too big, too strong, too close. "What the hell is your problem?"

"Your sister."

"Naomi?" Bradley's voice was choked with rage, his hands balled into fists. "You honestly think she's the problem when you're the one who has conveniently inserted herself right in the middle of warring societies? You're the one who Alistair called twenty times the night he died. You're the one who left your friend in a burning chapel."

He unleashed the torrent of words on me, spitting out all of his anger along with them, and before I even knew what I was doing, my hand went crashing down across his face, the sound of skin slapping skin echoing through the walls of the cabin. Bradley's entire body went tense and my knees went weak. I should run. I knew I should run. But I couldn't seem to get my legs to move. Instead, I stood completely still.

"Kate? Kate? Are you in there? Siegfried needs…" My dad's voice trailed off when he saw me standing in front of Bradley. "Right, hope I'm not interrupting something." My dad stumbled over his words, his eyes focused on the ceiling, and then finally settling back on us. "Actually, scratch that. I'm completely okay with interrupting whatever *this* is."

"She was just leaving," Bradley said, the words finding their mark on my heart.

My dad grabbed my arm and guided me toward the door. "It's past curfew. I suggest you pack your bag and go to bed, Bradley."

Thank God my dad didn't ask me any questions on the walk back to our cabin, because there was no way I'd have been able to string together any type of answer.

Because I was wrong about going back to Pemberly Brown with nothing. Everything that had happened at Camp Brown was something. But it was all so broken and disjointed, with sharp edges that cut. I had never felt more alone. So alone that I reached over to find my dad's hand. I squeezed it like I used to when I was little and in need of some reassurance. He squeezed back, our secret signal that everything was going to be okay, that I was safe.

But tonight, nothing could make me feel safe. Not even my dad.

Chapter 34

Kate?"

In my dream, time was erased and my hair was brown. Liam stood over me with kind eyes more blue than gray and a dimpled smile. And he repeated my name. It sounded right.

"Kate?"

This time, my body shook with the sound.

"Kate?"

When I opened my eyes, they might as well have been closed it was so dark. But Liam's face was close enough to distinguish, a breath away, his lips inches from my own.

"I need help. Porter's missing," he said, raising a finger to his lips so I knew to be quiet. It wasn't time to freak out or get Porter in trouble. It was no secret he didn't want to come here. He'd spent the bulk of the time drinking out of some water bottle. He was probably getting high with the maintenance crew. But we needed to find him. Ms. D. was depending on me to keep an eye on him.

We tiptoed out of the cabin and ran as soon as we hit the grass.

"We have to go to the lake," Liam called over his shoulder. Clouds had moved in, snuffing out the stars and masking the moon in a veil. It was darker. Dangerous. Liam was ahead now, closing in on the shore desperately. He knew something. He was scared.

"Porter!" He screamed his name, his voice carried by the breeze. "Porter!" he screamed again.

"Liam!" It was my turn to scream. "What's happening?" My eyes were wild, searching the water for movement.

Liam didn't answer, but instead ripped off his T-shirt and flung his flip-flops aside. He handed me a thick note card before screaming Porter's name into the blackness again. A light flickered on back at camp, and my hands shook as I looked down at the Factum Virtus I already knew was coming.

> The rocks are jagged, the lake deep. Face your death but save your-
> self. Make your Brother proud or lose him forever.

By now, every cabin was illuminated, and chaperones were sprinting to the lake's edge. Liam had disappeared beneath the water, and I wondered how much more I could possibly lose.

And then chaos. Voices. Fear. Confusion. Panic. Seven minutes. An eternity.

It took Liam, my Econ teacher, and Luca, Siegfried's assistant, to free Porter from between the sharp-edged boulders that lined the south edge of the shore. Everyone stood back as his chest was pumped, as Luca listened for a heartbeat and Liam wrapped a T-shirt around Porter's head to stop the bleeding. A collective breath was released when the heartbeat was found. I collapsed onto the sand, my body shaking violently in the aftermath that was all too reminiscent of the fire that had killed my best friend. Porter was whisked away to be cared for, and questions burst into the night.

Who found him? Why did he leave? What was he doing? How did you know?

And finally…*what is that?* Naomi pointed to the thick piece of paper I held between my shaking fingers.

"I found it," Liam said, running a hand through his wet hair. "I woke up and Porter was gone. This was sitting on his pillow. I got Kate and we came here."

Naomi narrowed her eyes. "It's another Factum Virtus," she announced, her eyes trained on Liam. "Thank God you woke up in the middle of the night, Liam. Thank God you knew where to look."

She spoke the words, and understanding struck me like a ton of bricks. I could see where this was going, and it made me dizzy.

I shook my head. "No, you don't understand. Liam was watching Porter. He…"

Some kid on the red team interrupted me, his squeaky voice like nails on a chalkboard. "I saw those notes in his bag. The Factum-whatevers. He had a bunch of them." He pointed a scrawny finger at Liam, and I knew no matter what I said, everything would all come falling down.

And it did. With Liam at the center. They pointed their fingers. They had their guy. The guy who never would have been standing in the middle if it hadn't been for me. The guy fighting everyone else's battles but his own.

"It's late." My dad spoke the words with new authority as he rested his hand on my shoulder. "Everyone needs to go back to camp. Porter is being cared for, and it's late and we'll find out more tomorrow."

Slowly everyone scattered back to camp.

Bradley hesitated by the dunes, as though he had something important to say, but ended up shaking his head and walking away without uttering a word. Seth looked like he was about to cry, but he wasn't in the business of breaking rules and he wasn't about to break my dad's. Maddie followed. Finally, only Liam and I were left.

The worst part was that Liam didn't even say anything. I deserved to be yelled at for forcing him into this mess, but he just stood there defeated.

"I'm so sorry, Liam."

He shook his head and was still scary quiet. A jolt of fear struck my stomach.

"You're sorry?" He said it and made a laughing, choking sound. "Do you have any idea what this has been like for me, Kate? You break up with me and start running around with Bradley-freaking-Farrow. And then you expect me to help you on another one of your insane quests to put an end to the societies that are supposedly destroying our school."

He was closing in on me, subconsciously moving closer with each word, face red, eyes shiny. "But wait, wait! There's more. You decide to go ahead and join the very society you're trying to destroy. And somehow it's my fault when another kid ends up hurt."

His face was just inches from mine now. I could feel his breath hot on my lips. "And not only that. No," he scary-laughed some more. "No, then you stand there with a blank face when I'm accused of picking off ex-Brotherhood members. Classic." The sarcasm was palpable.

Rage flooded my veins and made my feet tingle.

"You're kidding, right? What about you and Bethany? Was that my fault too? Did I force you to kiss her? Force you to flirt with her on the bus? She follows you around everywhere and it's so obvious you're together. Who the hell do you think you're kidding?"

My words were cut off by Liam's mouth crushing down on mine. He kissed me like he wanted to save me, to pull me back from whatever ledge I'd climbed out on. And for the first time in forever, it felt good to be saved. I clung to him like a life preserver, our bodies sealed so tight that there was no room left for anger or blame, just the raw energy of this one, amazing kiss.

"What the hell?"

It wasn't hard to recognize the voice that called out behind us. The way it sounded cracked and hoarse with grief, I knew it could only belong to Bradley.

I pulled away from Liam and turned around to try to explain.

"Bradley!" But he was already running down the beach at full speed, too far to hear the words that floated after him. I thought about chasing him, but I knew there was no way I'd ever be able to catch up. Not sure I wanted to after what he'd said to me earlier that night.

I stood there for a beat. Watching Bradley disappear into the black night, not ready to turn around and face Liam. Kissing him had felt amazing, but it didn't change anything. Not really. And I had no idea where we were supposed to go from there.

"Kate…" Liam put his hand on my shoulder, but I shook it off.

"I can't do this." I didn't turn around. I couldn't risk seeing the hurt on his face; I couldn't bear to watch him walk away. I wasn't ready to be rescued. I wasn't ready to forgive or be forgiven. Not until I finished what I'd started.

I sat down in the sand and pulled my knees up to my chin and watched the water lap gently onto the beach and then back out into the lake. Finally, the sound of Liam's footsteps faded and I was alone. Truly alone. I'd pushed myself to this place, and I deserved the pain that accompanied it.

Some of the clouds had dispersed, and the moon's reflection rippled on water that was dangerously smooth compared to what it had been just minutes before. And then my eye landed on something that didn't belong on the beach, something bright and shiny and foreign. An orange bottle nestled into the sand.

Orange. Grace's favorite color. It called to me from its spot on the dunes in the moonlight. I couldn't help but think how she would have stuck a big, pink gerbera daisy inside and arranged it on her windowsill. Even in the cool night air, I could feel the warmth of her smile.

As I walked toward the bottle, it became clear that it wasn't just some plastic piece of junk. It was actually quite beautiful. Heavy and intricate in my hands. I held it up toward the moon to make out the patterns etched into the glass and saw that there was a piece of paper inside.

A message in an orange bottle.

I shouldn't have been surprised to see her handwriting. I should have expected it to be from her. But the loopy words written in Grace's unmistakable cursive turned my muscles to mush. I fell hard onto the damp sand, my hands shaking, the meager light of the moon almost making it impossible to read the words.

Chapter 35

From Grace Lee's Journal—September 12

She's always at the chapel. Waiting for me. Naomi isn't at all what I expected her to be. She knows so much about the Sisterhood and the societies and our school. It's kind of unbelievable that all of this stuff has been going on for decades and no one really knows about any of it.

They have a vision, a plan, and I'm a part of it. Me. For the first time ever, someone thinks I'm smart enough, cool enough, amazing enough to actually do something important. They have been fighting for years, but now it's time for unity and I'm the key. The person who will finally make sure Conventus happens. An end to the war and the beginning of a new era.

Kate and Maddie have no idea what's going on. They're too busy chasing Bradley and Alistair and jockeying for a position at the right lunch table and all of that other first-year bullshit that used to seem so important.

But I have a purpose. A role. I'll be there in the basement on the night of initiation. Naomi told me to wait for him. Sometimes I giggle thinking about it. Would Kate be jealous if she knew that the boy she's been chasing will be coming for me? Sometimes I love imagining the look on her face when she finds out that I spent the night alone with her crush in the basement of the chapel. Just me, Bradley, and a secret plan that will change the history of our school forever. It's all up to us now. That's what Naomi said. It's all up to me.

Chapter 36

If my hands had been shaking before, now they were in full-on tremor mode. I held the truth crumpled between my fingers, and I had been right all along. Not one enemy but two. Two people who I had grown to trust. Two betrayals for the price of one.

And Grace. Her words stung. Was that really who I'd been? Some giggling first-year with a stupid crush? Is that really how she saw me? I wanted to call her and scream. I wanted to be able to defend myself. I wanted to run back to camp and tackle Bradley and Naomi and drag them back to Pemberly Brown where they'd be arrested for all the pain and anguish they'd caused so many people.

I wanted impossible things. So instead, I closed my eyes and I fell. I fell back to that place, to brown hair and changing leaves and possibility. I saw Bradley for the first time and felt my heart flutter when he smiled his dimpled smile. I heard cheers erupt in the bleachers of our stadium during football games and was overwhelmed by the scent of Pemberly Brown's expensive hallways.

I remembered that feeling of entitlement. The idea that I *deserved* everything I'd been given, that the universe somehow owed it to me. I'd like to think I'd changed, that I'd grown into someone with a better understanding of how things at Pemberly Brown worked, of how things in my world worked. But all I felt was bitterness. Maybe the only thing that had truly changed was the resentment that clung to me like smoke.

"Your dad sent me. It's almost 4 a.m., Kate." Seth's voice made me automatically crumple the paper further and kick sand over the beautiful bottle at my feet. "You have to come back." Seth shifted his weight from foot to foot. "It's not your fault. You know that, right? They warned everyone about night swimming. The lake gets deep fast and it's too easy to lose your bearings," Seth said. The kindness in his eyes made me want to die. I didn't deserve it. I was too dumb for kindness.

"I know. It's just…first Alistair and then Clayton and now Porter. God, I'm just such an idiot."

"Why are you doing this to yourself? None of this is your fault, Kate. You have all these people who love you," his voice cracked a little, "but it's like you're too busy punishing yourself to even notice."

I couldn't tell him that I deserved to be punished. I couldn't explain how stupid it was for anyone to consider loving me. So instead, I just followed silently in his footsteps as we padded back to camp.

Chapter 37

I felt better in the morning when we received word that Porter was recovering. And when we loaded the bus, Liam was on it. Even though he probably hated me, I was relieved to see him. Surely if he really was being accused of planting the Factum Virtus, someone would have come for him by now. I boarded the bus with more baggage, both figurative and literal, than I'd left with at the start of the week.

I had no idea what to think anymore, and I felt myself slipping into shutdown mode when I looked at Liam, Bradley, Naomi, even Seth and Maddie who squeezed into a seat together toward the back. I couldn't work out how everyone fit together, couldn't understand even the most subtle connection between Alistair, Clayton, and now Porter.

Maybe everyone was right. Maybe it was time to give up and move on, let other people clean up these messes. But all I could think about was getting called to another emergency meeting, seeing some terrible message on Amicus, watching my parents shrivel under the news of one more tragedy. And then I found myself right back where I started. But for now, with everyone crammed on the bus, Liam was safe, we all were safe, and that had to count for something.

I just wished I hadn't ever found Grace's message.

I felt a slight tug on my bright red hair and turned to find Naomi peeking through the crack in the bus seat.

"Hey," she said. Her face was unreadable. "I have no idea what's going on, but I want you to know that I'm here for you. Everyone is. We all just want to help."

Right, I thought. *Just as soon as you achieve Conventus.*

"Liam has nothing to do with any of this, Naomi. Just leave him out of it. Please, just leave him alone." My dad's head bobbed in the seat we shared. Most people were dozing after the crazy events of the previous night stole everyone's sleep. I was wide awake.

"You just…I just wish you understood, but you never can, Kate. Everything is so complicated, and I know this stuff with Liam doesn't make it any easier, but you have to take a step back. For you."

She had to be kidding. I raised my eyebrows and nodded. So that's how she wanted to play. A quote from Grace's journal entry was on the tip of my tongue, but I wasn't ready to tip my hand just yet. At this point, I wanted Naomi to think I was a complete idiot.

"Yeah, maybe you're right."

She smiled and started gathering up her stuff. We were home. Well, almost home anyway.

And that's when I saw it.

When we pulled down the lane onto Pemberly Brown's main campus, I blinked in rapid succession, willing the scene in front of me to dissipate like fog.

I blinked again.

I was seeing things. I had to be seeing things.

But it was still there.

A police car parked in front of the school, silent and ominous.

Maybe there was a break-in at the school. Or maybe it was just an alumnus stopping by to walk through campus. Maybe someone had pulled the fire alarm or dialed in a bomb threat.

But deep down I knew the truth, and when I saw Ms. D. standing next to the uniformed officer, it was confirmed.

The bus rolled to a stop, and moments later, the police officer and Ms. D. were talking to the driver and then making an announcement.

"Everyone please stay seated." The police officer's voice rang with quiet authority. "Liam Gilmour?" My stomach dropped when Ms. D. called his name. This couldn't be happening. Porter was wrong. This was a huge mistake. It had to be.

I pushed out of my seat and up the aisle to explain. "Wait!" I shouted to no one. To everyone.

"Miss, I'm sorry, but you need to go back to your seat

immediately." The police officer's hand squeezed my shoulder just a little too hard.

"But you don't understand. I need to talk to Ms…er… Headmistress Bower. I need to explain. Liam isn't the person she's looking for. I just need more time."

The policeman gave me a stern look and then turned to my father. "Please control this student."

"Yes, sir." My dad's arm snaked across my lap like a seat belt.

"What the hell do you think you're doing?" he hissed. "This is why you're always in trouble, Kate. I know you care about Liam, but you need to let him fight his own battles."

Tears sprung in my eyes as I watched Liam walk slowly up to the front of the bus, only to be led outside into the waiting police car with Ms. D.

The problem was that Liam wasn't in trouble for fighting his own battles. He was in trouble for fighting mine.

Chapter 38

It's amazing how slowly time goes when you're waiting for something to happen. I locked myself in my room the second we got home from our ridiculous camping trip. I couldn't believe that I had failed so many people I cared about so miserably.

Liam was in serious trouble, and it was all my fault.

I had to do something, but there was no way I was getting out of the house tonight. I had heard my father whispering to my mom about my behavior on the bus. They had gone into full lockdown mode. My cell phone was charging on their nightstand, the house alarm was set, my dad was camped out on the couch, and my mom was supposedly working in her bedroom, but I knew the truth. They were watching me. Policing me like a couple of parole officers. Of all the nights for them to take an interest in my safety, I cursed them for choosing this one.

And so I sat up all night staring at my alarm clock. Willing the seconds to pass so I could leave for school. Willing the minutes to speed by so I could figure out a way to get to Liam. Willing the hours to dwindle so I could do something aside from sit here completely worthless.

Not that I had any idea how I was going to fix everything, but I knew where I had to start. The Farrows.

Morning bled into night, and it was finally time for me to leave for school. My parents watched me walk toward the bus stop, all bathrobes and nerves. I waved at them as I turned the corner, finally out of their sight.

I felt the presence of the car before it even got to my side. It was black, more Batmobile than sedan, all tinted windows and fancy finishes. It slowed to a stop, and I heard Ms. D.'s voice.

"We need to talk."

"Thank God." I pulled my book bag from my shoulders so I could slide into the car.

Ms. D. had on her usual uniform of all black except for a pair of shocking red pumps. Even her glasses were black-rimmed. An open newspaper rested in her lap and a slash of red lipstick lined the rim of her coffee mug. I searched her face for signs of the security guard who had once been the only adult I trusted at PB, but all traces of her had been wiped away with tasteful makeup and careful styling.

"I'm sure Liam's arrest must have come as a shock." Ms. D. did not look up from the newspaper, but did offer a flick of her eyebrows.

I dug my fingernails into the soft leather of the seat beneath me.

"You have the wrong guy. The Farrows…"

Ms. D. cut me off with a wave of her hand.

"The Farrows have nothing to do with this, Kate. We have a witness who saw Liam leave the letter on Porter's bed. And we found additional letters when we searched his bag from the trip."

"Who?" But I already knew the answer. It was Bradley or Naomi. It had to be. They were the only ones with a motive.

"No one ever said this would be easy, Kate. You lost your best friend. All around you, life continues on, but she's still gone. It gets better, but it never gets easy." Ms. D. finally looked up from the paper but not toward me. Her eyes narrowed a bit as she spoke, fixed on the window and Pemberly Brown's drifting campus.

"Who's the witness?" I ignored her poetic summation of my life the same way she'd ignored my question the first time I asked.

She sighed then and folded her newspaper crisply onto her lap. "You know I can't tell you that, Kate."

"Then let me out. Now. I'll figure it out myself."

"I'm sorry, but I can't do that either." The car suddenly grew dark.

"Wait…what's…" I scooted toward the window to get a closer look. It was morning; the sun was just making its brilliant debut. My heart came to life in my chest, one beat right on top of the next. "Where are we going?" The car felt half its size now, the dark walls closing in against me, the leather suffocating. My eyes barely adjusted enough to make out the tips of Ms. D.'s blood-red toes. This was not good. I considered how long it would take for someone to realize I had been kidnapped.

I no longer had friends, so that eliminated the school day. My parents worked 'til God only knew when, so that eliminated after school, and I often missed my parents all together in the morning, so that eliminated tomorrow. It could be weeks. I felt the car closing in.

"I expect a lot out of you. Everyone does. But it's only because we know you're capable of great things, Kate."

Not if I'm dead, I thought, my heart practically clawing up my esophagus. The car moved slower now, and goose bumps erupted along my arms that no amount of frantic rubbing would squelch. Not only did the sides of the car reduce to the size of a shoebox, but the blackened world outside had split itself in two. We were driving through some sort of tunnel, which was impossible because there were no tunnels where we lived. Not one.

"I wouldn't choose anyone else." Ms. D. continued her bizarre diatribe, which only added to my distress. "You are a leader, Kate. Your friends can't get the job done. They can't even be trusted. But you're different. You're focused. You remind me of…" The car came to a stop, and a faint series of beeps could be made out on the driver's side.

And then light. Not a lot of it, not natural, normal, I'm-not-going-to-die-after-all sunlight, but a soft glowing light that illuminated Ms. D.'s face. We moved a few more feet until the car stopped, parked inside the weird tunnel that I never knew existed.

"You remind me of me." Ms. D. pulled on the latch to open the door and stood outside the car waiting for me to do the same. It was as though she were asking me in which place I'd rather die. Inside the car or out. I looked around at the expensive black leather and tinted windows. It didn't look at all like the kidnapper vans from my imagination. But I wasn't taking any chances. I slid out after Ms. D.

The space was lined with bricks, and it only took me a second to place it. I *did* know tunnels. I just didn't know cars could drive down into them. But of course they could. At least, of course Ms. D.'s could.

"I hope you don't mind the impromptu meeting. We have a bit of celebrating to do before school."

The sharp heels of Ms. D.'s pumps clicked along the stone floor, reverberating off the curved walls. The great wooden door loomed ahead, and it struck me how I could still be surprised by Pemberly Brown. Every shock that I swore would be my last was always followed by something even more ridiculous or crazy. I shook my head at the thought, accepting it, embracing it. I was bound to be one of those crazy girls later in life who desperately searched for the excitement of her youth. I was so totally screwed.

"So you accept?" Ms. D. rested her palm beside the intricate carving of the Sisterhood's seal.

My eyebrows pulled in confusion. Accept my death? Accept the fact that Liam is going to be punished for a crime he didn't commit? Accept the fact that I'm a complete failure?

Apparently Ms. D. took my confusion as a yes because she

pushed open the door. And then came clapping. Dozens of hands pounding together, smiling faces, girls rising up and clapping. Celebrating. I scanned the crowd and saw Taylor and Bethany. Taylor smiling, Bethany scowling. Nothing new there. I searched for Naomi Farrow. I wanted to see if she'd meet my eye. I wanted to find the truth in them.

But she was nowhere to be found.

Ms. D. cocked her head toward mine, her red lips poised beside my ear. "I've decided you should be our next leader. Your drive, your passion. You're unstoppable, Kate."

Unstoppable. What a joke. I was constantly being stopped, blocked, thwarted.

"This is a new era, Kate," Ms. D. continued. "And it all starts with you."

Chapter 39

The school day seemed endless. Bradley, Naomi, and Liam were all noticeably absent. And me, I was there. Physically, I mean. Mentally, I was interrogating Porter. I was digging through the files in the Farrow family office. I was with Liam. Begging him to forgive me. Figuring out a way to get him off.

"Kate!" It was a familiar squeak. A squeak I had come to love. "Did you hear? Liam! Expelled!" Panic was written all over Seth's red face. It would have been comic if the situation hadn't been so serious.

"What? Expelled? Are you sure?" I knew it was bad and I figured Liam would be in trouble, but to be expelled so quickly. I guess I just thought we'd have more time. But as usual, it wasn't on my side.

"I'm sure. I just saw the paperwork in the office." Seth was almost running to keep up with me as I blazed through the hallway toward the office.

"Wait! Kate! Stop!" Seth grabbed my arm and swung me around to face him. Turns out he was, like, freakishly strong.

"Let me go. I'll talk to her. I'll fix this. You don't understand, Seth. She'll listen to me now."

"You're not thinking straight. You're smarter than this, Kate." Seth grabbed me by the shoulders and stared straight into my eyes. "If you go in there now and cause a huge scene, Ms. D.'s gonna be on to you." He steered me away from the office. "But if you lie low, if you can get close enough, you can strike from within."

God, he was right. It was my plan all along. To join the Sisterhood and become one of them, and here I was, their new leader. Ms. D. trusted me. I could do more for Liam from the inside.

"I hate to interrupt this little chat." Bethany's tone belied her words as she practically hip-checked Seth to plant herself directly in between us. "But we're having a sleepover in the headquarters." She held up a tattered duffel bag that hadn't seen the light of day since my last sleepover with Grace and Maddie.

"But my parents…"

"Where'd you think I got the bag?" Bethany smiled evilly, and I couldn't even imagine what kind of lies had been told to make this happen. My guess it had at least required a call from Ms. D.

I looked at Seth. He jerked his head in a subtle nod and I slapped a smile on my face. Game on.

• • •

"So this is where the magic happens!" Taylor splayed her arms out like a game-show hostess showcasing a row of computers, screens flashing in the darkness.

"Oh, um, cool." Leave it to the Sisterhood to turn a slumber party into a surveillance operation.

Taylor grabbed my hand. "Come on, you're going to love this."

She gestured breezily at some girls sitting in front of the computers, and they moved aside instantly. I couldn't help but wonder if anyone would ever obey me like that. Somehow I didn't think so. In high school, obedience was usually earned with charm and good looks. I was average on both counts. But maybe it didn't matter if I had someone like Taylor to do my dirty work for me.

"So, this is it. Our command center." Taylor yanked me down into the chair next to her. Flashing before us were five screens positioned at different exits at Liam's house. "We're watching his every move. No more surprises."

I wanted to laugh because it was so ridiculous to think that Liam was involved. But I kept my face composed, my emotions in check. I couldn't show any sign of weakness, or I'd blow my cover.

Her fingers tapped and clicked on the screen until she pulled up Liam's email account. "And we're monitoring all of his email activity, as well. He isn't going to hurt anyone else." She grabbed my hand and squeezed. "All thanks to you."

Movement on one of the monitors caught my eye. Liam walked outside onto his patio and collapsed into a chair. Watching him sit outside while I viewed him from an underground tunnel made me a little queasy. This was so wrong. But I couldn't let on. Not yet.

"So we're just going to watch him now? I thought we had all of the information we needed. I mean, he's already been kicked out of school."

"I know, but I guess Ms. D. suspects there was someone else involved. Some of the timing just does not add up."

"So we're just supposed to sit here and wait for him to get in contact with his partner in crime?" I couldn't tear my eyes away from the screen. Liam's shoulders were hunched over, his head in his hands. *Oh God, he must hate me so much.*

"That's the idea." Taylor smirked.

"But what about Naomi?" The words came out of my mouth too fast. I couldn't stop them.

"Naomi?" Taylor's pretty features twisted in confusion.

"I mean…is she okay? I haven't seen her all day."

Taylor's face relaxed. "Oh yeah, you lost me for a second there. She's fine. Just sick. Stomach flu or something."

Stomach flu, my ass. The Farrows were planning something. They had to be. And I had to stop them before anyone else got hurt.

Taylor snapped her fingers, and the first-years appeared behind us in seconds. "I'm exhausted. Let's go get some rest while they keep an eye on things. Delegation is the key, my friend."

"Oh, right. Delegation." Leadership 101 with Taylor Wright. Good times.

I didn't protest when she grabbed my hand. I did look back, though, for a second and saw the first-years hovered around the computer, giggling as they scrolled through Liam's personal emails.

A combination of curiosity and horror rushed through me as I watched them click on an email from Bethany.

> You keep saying that you aren't interested, but I can't stop thinking about you.

Wait, so Liam wasn't into Bethany? Was it possible that their whole love affair had been one-sided?

"Aren't you coming?" Taylor asked, her light eyebrows pulled together.

"Oh…um, yeah." I wanted to sit down next to the girls and pour over all of those emails, but it would have been so wrong, such a huge violation of Liam's privacy. But as Taylor led me toward a suite at the end of the hall, the words of the email kept running through my mind.

I needed a plan. Now that I was finally here, there had to be proof that Naomi and Bradley were behind this whole thing. I just needed to figure out how to get to it.

Once I was sure that almost everyone was asleep, I got up and made my way back to the computers. If they had hacked into Liam's emails, there must be a way to get into Naomi and Bradley's. As I padded down the hall toward the bay of computers, I was relieved to see that the first-years had given up their watch. There was no one in sight.

I sat down in front of the monitor. Liam's emails were still up on the screen. Before I could stop myself, I had already opened one he'd sent to Bethany.

> Please stop writing, stop calling, stop kissing me. I still have feelings for someone else. It has nothing to do with you, but I just can't offer you anything more than friendship at this point.

My breath caught in my throat. Liam still had feelings for someone else. The email was from a week ago. Had that someone been me? Probably. Too bad he probably hated me now.

My hands shook a little on the keyboard and I closed my eyes. *Not now, Kate. Focus.* I navigated to the main menu, and sure enough, there was a list of every student at Pemberly Brown. I pulled up Bradley's name and clicked on an email he sent to Naomi earlier today.

> N—The Chapel. 2 AM. This happens tonight. Now or never.

It read like a dare, and there was no way I wasn't going to take it.

Chapter 40

There wasn't time to think about how the long shadows stretching across the cool brick in the tunnels looked like crooked fingers or that the temperature was five degrees cooler underground, like in a morgue. I didn't even have time to think whether or not I would be safe with Ms. D.'s driver by myself or if it was even legal for him to take me anywhere.

I knocked on the window frantically and even through the tinted glass could see the driver jolt awake, grabbing at his chest. I widened my eyes, praying he'd recover. The last thing I needed was to give the poor guy a heart attack.

He rolled down the window, his chest rising and falling faster than it should have been.

"I'm sorry if I woke you," I said uncomfortably. I wondered if he always had to sleep in the car or if he switched off with another driver. Either way, kind of the worst job ever unless living in a car was your thing. Time to focus. "Do you mind driving me somewhere, Mr…?" I blushed at not knowing what to call him. I hated that.

"You can call me Judd. And that's what I'm here for, Ms. Lowry." The driver gestured to the back of the car with kind eyes. Great. Nothing made me feel less competent than when someone remembered my name and I had totally forgotten theirs.

"Thanks, Mr…Judd." His eyes crinkled around the corners even deeper, and I climbed in the back as he started the car and rolled down the privacy window. I resisted the urge to launch my body through the opening and into the front seat. I settled on shoving my head through and breathing down his neck instead.

"Where to?" Judd drove the car forward and punched in a code that opened a secret garage door. Black night spilled in. I glanced down at the two dots on my phone inching forward on the screen.

"The chapel. Can you drop me by the gardens?"

"Not a problem, my dear." Judd tapped his fingers on the steering wheel as he drove. "But if you don't mind me asking, what are you doing out here all alone in the middle of the night?" He caught my eye in the rearview mirror, and I thought of Liam. This was it. My chance to save him. To make things right.

My stomach muscles tightened as we closed in on the gardens. I hated the thought of going near the chapel by myself at night. It was haunted. At least for me it was. Going there alone would mean facing everything that had happened to Grace. I couldn't go alone. My body felt rooted to the seat of the car.

"My daughter's barely ten but acts about seventeen. I'd kill her if she ever got involved in this stuff." His eyes flicked to mine in the rearview mirror. "But I'm not stupid." Judd twisted around in his seat. "Here." He held out a small container of pepper spray. Such a dad move. "I'll wait for ten minutes, but if you're not back, I'll come looking. Call me immediately if you need me before that."

I looked down at my phone, willing myself to move. Judd's number appeared on the screen. Was I prepared for what I might find? Did they sneak to the chapel in the middle of the night to do séances or sacrifices or pray to some great Conventus god or something? Were they planning another attack?

It was enough to give me the courage to get out of the car and face whatever was waiting for me.

"This might take longer than ten minutes, but I'll hurry." I shut the door with a soft thud and never felt more alone.

The air was still crisp at this hour, and it cut through my thin sweater as I ran the path toward the thick woods beyond. I gripped the pepper spray in one palm, the tube slipping with sweat despite the cold air, while my phone was clenched in the other. Anticipation bubbled in my chest, burning my lungs, and the air felt charged with the brink of a discovery. Justice and an ending all rolled into one. I'd catch Naomi and Bradley, and this would all be over. Everyone could move on, and no one would get hurt again. Happily ever after. The end.

I slowed at the entrance to the woods and let the thick trees and heavy undergrowth take my breath away for a second. If I thought it was black outside, I didn't know the definition. The woods swallowed things whole, and I wasn't sure they'd ever spit me back out. But with responsibility came great risks, and I was ready. *Mind over matter*, I thought as I willed my feet to tread lightly. Like eating sushi or swimming with sharks. This wasn't only where Grace died, it was where she'd been betrayed and tricked. It was where she'd been sacrificed. And now it was going to be the place where she was avenged.

Movement caught my eye, although in their camouflage clothing Naomi and Bradley were almost impossible to make out. Naomi held a white card, and it cut through the night, glaring at me. Daring me. They were delivering another one of their horrible Factum Virtutes. I'd actually caught them in the act. With shaking hands, I brought my phone to life and let my finger hover over a single button.

I snapped the picture and immediately sent it off to the entire Sisterhood. They'd come now. All of them. They'd panic. But it would all be worth what everyone was about to witness.

I should wait for them to arrive so we could all confront them together, but I remembered the way Naomi had accused Liam. The way she'd framed him. And I just couldn't stop myself from speaking the two words that had been waiting on the tip of my tongue since I'd found out Grace had died.

"It's over."

Chapter 41

H ow could you?" The words erupted from my mouth in staccato. For a minute, they both just stared at me, but it wasn't until Naomi let herself fall to the ground, her small frame shaking with tears, that I knew I'd won. I'd finally won.

Bradley wrapped his arm around her and tried to shush her, and I had to look away. The moment was so private and so real, and it was messing with my head. They'd set up Liam, they'd orchestrated the deadly Factum Virtutes, but even worse, they'd killed Grace. All of those secret meetings, the way they'd instructed her to wait in the basement no matter what. The way they'd preyed on her feeling lost and confused and used all of those emotions to make her feel like she was important, like she belonged. They didn't deserve to be human, to act sad. I wanted them to be the kind of villains with twirling mustaches and evil plans. I needed to be able to hate them.

And in that moment, I stopped. I stopped and I remembered Grace. The way her long black hair always dried perfectly straight. The way she always started laughing at the most inappropriate times. Her ridiculous plans and ideas and the way she could pretty much talk anyone into anything. I remembered the way she used to snore like an eighty-year-old man at every sleepover we ever had together and how she'd granted me permission to kick her repeatedly until she rolled over onto her stomach. How we knew we'd be friends through college, through marriage and babies and midlife crises and lunch dates and old age. How we didn't have to talk about it, but that our friendship was rooted in forever.

And there it was. The rest of our lives. I had thought I'd be kicking her sorry ass until we were little old ladies bunking together in a nursing home. And the Farrows had stolen that from me. They'd stolen my best friend.

"How could you have let her die out here? Alone? How could you go to her funeral and pretend to cry? How could you live with yourself after what you've done?" My words all ran together like the lines of mascara that were streaking down Naomi's cheeks. She was sobbing uncontrollably now, and Bradley was still buried in her shoulder, but that didn't stop me. Nothing could have stopped me. Not even the sound of footsteps approaching behind me.

"You killed her. You killed a girl in cold blood. You killed your best friend." The words came out like a curse. "And for what? Your asinine little society? For some half-baked dream of unity? I don't care who your parents are. I don't care how much money you have. I will spend the rest of my life ending yours."

Somewhere behind me, a small spattering of applause broke out. I had an audience. The entire Sisterhood flanked my sides. Headmistress D. and her driver stood back, watching with interest. It was too dark to be sure, but I was almost positive she was nodding encouragingly.

"You don't think we know?" Naomi's words were barely audible, choked with tears and muffled by her brother's arm. She surprised me by pulling away from Bradley and making her way shakily to her feet. "You think I haven't spent the past 392 days thinking these exact same things? You think I haven't wanted to die?" As she stood, her voice grew stronger, her words more pronounced.

"Bullshit," I spat. "What total bullshit. How can you even say that with a straight face?"

"You have no idea what you're talking about, Kate. None." Bradley chimed in now. "You don't know what we've been through, the things we've thought about doing…" His voice cracked, and he looked back toward the remains of the chapel.

"Actually, Bradley, I know exactly what you have thought about doing. Even worse, I know what you've done. You killed your best friend. You've been targeting the Brotherhood one by one, forcing them to pay for not supporting Conventus."

"Wait, what are you even talking about?" Bradley looked genuinely shocked, but I wasn't fooled.

I shook the letter at him. "Nice try, but I have the proof. I read Grace's journal. Why do you think I'm out here tonight? What did you think I was doing? I'm here for this. For one of your stupid Factum Virtutes. And I finally have it."

Naomi laughed, a hysterical, broken sound. And once she started, she couldn't stop. It was unsettling. She handed me the letter.

"Read it." She managed to choke out the words between her hysterics. "Go on. *Read it.*"

I looked back at Ms. D., and she nodded again. With trembling fingers, I opened the letter.

Dear Grace,

We haven't forgotten you. We haven't forgotten your sacrifice. This week, we sent your parents yellow peonies and made a donation to the animal protective league in your name. We remembered hearing something about how you rescued your dog from there, so that was our good deed this week. More soon.

Naomi's careful script was unmistakable. The letter wasn't proof of anything except two students trying to honor a dead classmate.

I lunged for Naomi, only to feel dozens of hands holding me back.

"What is this? What does it even mean? Where are the real letters? You framed Liam! You're lying." It was my turn for hysterics. I couldn't process how they had managed to trick me again. I couldn't fathom how two people could continue to get away with murder. Literally.

"It was our fault she died." Bradley's voice was steady. "We take full responsibility. She was waiting in the chapel basement for me. It was a test. We had to be sure about her allegiance to Conventus. We had to show her that the Sisterhood didn't care about her enough to save her." Bradley's face crumpled and he turned away. "It was my fault. I was supposed to go back for her, but the fire…" His voice dissolved into a cry that sounded like it was torn from his throat.

"We had no idea that Alistair was going to set the chapel on fire," Naomi choked out. "He was just supposed to create a distraction, and by the time we got there…" She stopped and looked at me, tears coursing down her cheeks again. "I am so sorry. You have no idea how sorry I am. You have no idea how many times I've wanted to die, to burn for this." The grief in her eyes was wild, real. I remembered that grief. I remembered what it was like to want to die.

"But we had nothing to do with Alistair, Clayton, or Porter. I swear." Bradley had regained his composure and his rich-boy mask was firmly back in place.

"You really expect us to believe you? After you killed Grace?" I expected to hear the rest of the Sisterhood cheer behind me. I expected Ms. D. to come forward and escort the Farrows back to her office. I expected the police.

"I think it's time for you to go home, Kate. I know you care for

Liam, but we have all the evidence we need at this point." Ms. D. said the words with quiet authority and turned back toward her car. My heart broke a little. My anger had been popped like an overinflated balloon, and now all that was left was sadness. Sadness that aside from the people here tonight, no one would ever know what really happened to Grace, but mostly sadness that it had taken me this long to realize that it didn't really matter.

Liam's life was ruined and it was all my fault. Grace was gone, and I was the one who had let her go. The common denominator here was me.

Chapter 42

My eyes burned with exhaustion, sadness, defeat, you name it. Bradley helped his sister up, and neither of them could meet my eye. Taylor wrung her hands until Bethany pulled her away without so much as a good-bye, and the rest of the girls followed suit.

I was alone with Judd's pepper spray and my phone. The past two years roiled deep inside of me, filling all the spaces where a normal person used to be. I wondered if this was what it felt like to be at a breaking point, because I felt like I was coming apart at the seams, sadness seeping out of my joints and tearing me apart.

Grinding my teeth, I turned in the direction of my house. The wind kicked up, pulling at my sweater and making the branches above creak and moan. Normally, my heart would thump in response and I'd become hyper aware of my surroundings just in case someone was after me, because there almost always seemed to be someone after me. But after everything with Bradley and Naomi, and Liam still in trouble for a crime he hadn't committed and a real killer still on the loose, none of it mattered anymore. I was back to square one, and the old recklessness was back in full force.

So when a car pulled up beside me at approximately 2:57 in the morning, I didn't pick up my pace or grab at my heart or grip the pepper spray until my knuckles were white and my fingers tingled. *I dare you. I dare you to mess with me, to try something, to hurt me any more than I am already hurt.* It wasn't possible.

"Kate?"

I knew that voice.

"Kate, get in. You shouldn't be out here alone." The wind cut through my sweater and wrapped around my waist and up my back. My teeth chattered. I was freezing. When I turned to the shiny, black BMW and saw Porter behind the wheel, I didn't hesitate. Porter with his sad eyes and his broken spirit. I got in because looking into his eyes was a little like looking into a mirror.

"Thank God I found you," he said, rubbing his jaw.

"Yeah, I guess."

"I'm sure you think I'm…like…unstable or something, and I guess everyone's right, but I'm not going to hurt you or anyone or anything." The words tumbled out of Porter's mouth, and I felt bad that he even felt like he had to say something. I knew none of it was his fault. If anyone knew better, it was me.

"I don't…"

"It's just…complicated," he interrupted. "Everything at the beach, being sent home…it's not what everyone thinks."

"It's okay, Porter. You don't have to explain. I get it." He didn't have to tell me about the messed-up nature of the Brotherhood. I already knew.

He pulled to a stop sign and lingered at the intersection. "I don't want to upset you, but I found something and I think you deserve to see it."

God, this had to be the last thing I needed right now. The only thing I *deserved* to see at this point was a padded cell where I could finally stop hurting myself and everyone else I happened to touch. Somehow deserving to see and destroying were almost always synonymous. I *deserved* to see that picture of Liam kissing Bethany. I *deserved* to hear Maddie saying terrible things about me. I *deserved* to find out that Taylor had punked me and sent me fake emails from Grace. But did I really? Had I somehow brought this all upon myself, starting with the night I'd abandoned my best friend?

I pursed my lips together to stop the question from spilling out.

Porter turned and reached into the backseat, holding a crumpled piece of paper when he twisted back around. He handed me the sheet, and when I saw the orange writing, its source was clear.

"I found it in the hallway crumpled against a locker. I didn't know if I should show you or not, but I knew if someone had something of Alistair's…" Porter's voice cracked on his brother's name, and tears flooded my eyes. He was so hurt, and there was nothing anyone could do about it. It was so unfair. I didn't even know what to say. All this time, I hated when people didn't know what to say, and I had no words.

"I'm…" I began lamely.

"Forget it. It's not a big deal." Porter shook his head and pulled away from the stop sign. I ran my fingers over the words, desperately wanting to read them, but knowing I should wait until I'd made it home behind my locked bedroom door.

"You should read that now. It's…I don't know. It's kind of, like, urgent."

I nodded, my eyes already skimming her loopy handwriting. Urgent. Even after her death, Grace still had a knack for delivering something right on time. I needed a sign, and Grace had given me one. Maybe I deserved to read this after all.

Chapter 43

I still can't believe that this is happening to me. I can't believe their lies. These societies want to destroy our school. They want to go back to the days of Pemberly and Brown. They want to separate me from the person I love the most.

I think about that when Cameron holds my hand. I love him. I can't lose him. We shouldn't have to lose people we love because of some stupid society. It's time to take action. It's time to destroy the societies for good. And anyone who's not with me, they're against me.

It was wrong. All wrong. There was no way Grace had written that. I looked closer at her Ls and Ys, at the angle of the words, and I closed my eyes, imagining the entries I had smoothed into my own notebook at home. Something didn't add up. Grace's feelings for Cameron would never have been expressed in this way. The paper was forged.

But why would someone go to the trouble of sending me Grace's actual journal entries only to lead up to one that's so clearly fake?

My eyes snapped up to Porter.

It's time to destroy the societies for good.

"Hey, I think you missed the turn…" The words came out in a hoarse whisper, and his only response was to push harder on the gas pedal. My body jolted back in the seat, and I felt the panic wind its way around my chest like a straitjacket.

"Porter? It's late and you're right, we really do need to talk, but maybe in the morning after I've had the chance to process…"

He jerked the steering wheel all the way to the right, taking a turn so fast that I was sure the tiny car would flip over. Something was wrong. So, so, so wrong. But it wasn't until I started to recognize the houses that I realized how wrong. It wasn't until we pulled into Grace's driveway that I stopped breathing. And it wasn't until I saw the soft glow from behind Grace's old window that everything went black. Grace's parents had moved away after the holidays, back to family, away from this broken town. The house sat dark and empty. Until now.

Chapter 44

I dug my fingernails into the soft leather of the seat, wondering if there was time for me to jump out of the car and run away. Porter's eyes focused on my hands.

"Don't be scared. It's not what you think. We just want to talk."

We? What did that even mean? Who was in there? My stomach heaved, and the roof of the car seemed to close in on me. I made a promise. I would stop everything, *everything* if someone, *anyone* would help me escape. I'd let Grace go. I'd listen to my parents. I'd be a better friend. Hell, I'd even make new friends. Anything if it meant I could get away from here.

Porter read my mind. "Don't run. Just…it's okay. I don't want to have to…" He looked up at the second story of the house. "Look, everything will make sense once you get inside." He clasped his fingers around my wrist hard enough to bruise. "I know how you feel, Kate. We have nothing left, and we're the only ones who can fix it. You know that, right?"

My throat narrowed. It was like I was breathing through a straw with a pea stuck in it. This couldn't be happening now, not when I needed strength to get away, not when I needed to save myself. But I knew the signs. I was panicking, and there was no way out but through. Blackness curled around the edge of my vision, and I watched Porter open his car door in slow motion. And then mine was open and I was being dragged out, his arm locked around mine. I knew I should run, but the world was fuzzy and pixilated, like being led through the broken back door of Grace's old house in a dream.

Walking through the door was like stepping back in time. My head was already spinning with my latest epiphany, but this was too much. My brain was on overload. Even though the Lees' house had been empty for months, it still smelled exactly the same. Like laundry detergent and burnt firewood. I was home.

In this kitchen, Grace and I had burned endless batches of chocolate chip cookies because we were too busy eating the raw dough to watch the timer. The old-school phone with one of those spiral cords still sat on the kitchen island. We used to drag it into the pantry and make the most ridiculous prank calls while her dog, Chewy, sat outside the door and whined for treats. The wallpaper was peeling and dust powdered every surface, but it was still Grace's house. It was still our home.

But it was too quiet. And the boy standing in the kitchen saying words I couldn't hear looked foreign and wrong. There were dirty paper plates scattered on the counter, empty pizza boxes piled in a corner, and crushed cans strewn in the sink. This house looked inhabited in all the wrong ways.

In a fog, Porter dragged me through the kitchen, into the foyer, and up the stairs where Grace's bedroom stood at the end of the hall. I heard her voice taunting me that it was too early to fall asleep, could see her poke her dark head out from behind the door while she changed into her pajamas.

Porter yanked on my arm, and the memory popped like a bubble as he pulled me down the dark hall toward the glow spilling from under Grace's old door. When he threw it open, I fully expected Grace to greet me with her cracked smile or at least her ghost lurking around the edges, returning to give me some sort of message, to help me get out of the mess I'd gotten myself into. What I got was Cameron Thompson.

Chapter 45

I hadn't seen Grace's crazy-ass boyfriend since the fall when he'd officially been expelled for being a drug-addled, crazy person. Honestly, can't say that I'd missed him much.

His face was dark with stubble, and the flickering candle in his hand made his eyes look black in their sockets. Wait, not just one candle, but hundreds, lining the floors, propped up on a bent wooden box, surrounding the window.

"Sorry about the lights. Not like I could call the electric company." Cameron laughed but it sounded more like a growl. "Good to see you again, my friend. We've been waiting for you to come around."

Being in Grace's room surrounded by candles and hearing Cameron speak was enough to lift me out of the haze of memories. What was out of focus before snapped crisply together, and I realized that there was a very real possibility that I might never make it out of Grace's house alive.

I stepped backward with my hands raised in surrender. "I...I want to leave. I need to get out of here right now." Porter blocked my path, and my back hit his front.

"Infiltrating the Sisterhood was genius, Kate. Genius," Cameron said, gripping my shoulders too hard. "I mean, you had everyone right where we wanted them."

I shrugged away from his touch, shivers raising the hairs on my arm like a rash.

"We tried to help you," he began, his glassy blue eyes wide and crazed. "The journal entries, those stupid cards getting the Brotherhood to off themselves. They were all reminders, Kate!" Cameron swayed on his feet and came dangerously close to knocking over a candle. I couldn't breathe. "It was *your* job. You promised to avenge her death. You were the only one who could honor her memory, and you failed."

The gravity of the words Cameron barked out at me settled on my shoulders like a metric ton. Cameron, the loser who had been MIA for at least four months, thought I was a failure? I wanted to laugh. And now he was back and thought that putting people in danger, *killing* people, was helping. And then it dawned on me. Alistair. They'd killed Alistair. How could Porter live with himself?

I spun around to face him. "How could you do that to your brother? How could you sit back and let him hurt himself? For what?" I could feel my face getting red, the blood rushing to my cheeks and spreading out. I felt dangerously close to tears, and all I wanted was to get the hell out of this place and make good on my promise to stay out of things from now on. I was done. Grace was gone, and I was done.

Porter's eyes flashed to Cameron's in silent desperation. "I… we…I just…he never let me in…he tortured me…it was just supposed to scare him." Porter stuttered through the broken explanation, taking steps back toward the door in defense. He lifted his hands. "I tried. I mean, I wanted to stop." He looked at Cameron then. Pleading. "Kate's right. It's time to go."

Cameron's face darkened, and he laughed even though nothing was remotely funny. "You think anyone will believe you, Porter? We've already been through this. If you back out now, I'll tell everyone you forced me to help you kill your brother." He raised his eyebrows. "I'll even throw in the ex-headmaster. Still feel like leaving?"

Porter began to backpedal then. "We didn't kill Alistair. Don't you see?" Porter leaned toward me, and I noticed how bloodshot his eyes were. "The Brotherhood killed him. He couldn't stand up to them. He could never say no. It doesn't matter who sent the Factum Virtus. His loyalty killed him the same way it killed Grace. It has to stop." I wondered how long Porter had been trying to convince himself of his innocence. He was wringing his hands like Lady-freaking-Macbeth. No way was he sleeping at night.

"So we're making a statement," Cameron said, running his fingers through his greasy hair. "Tonight. In this house. A letter has already been sent to the papers, and it's only a matter of time before it's picked up everywhere. People love a good story. *Tragic End in an*

Effort to Abolish Secret Societies. Man, that really has a nice ring to it, am I right?"

My mind was spinning. What kind of tragic end was Cameron referring to? I wished I could access my phone telepathically, send a message to Liam or Seth, Maddie, Naomi, or Bradley. My freaking parents. Anyone. I needed help.

"They'll have to do something. Shut down the societies, close the school, honor the dead. It's only fair," Porter continued.

Panic flared in my chest, and my hand reached for the phone in my pocket reflexively. But the movement set both of them off, and suddenly they were on me in a flash of arms and hands and elbows. My phone fell to the floor of Grace's bedroom, knocking a candle on the way. Hot wax pooled on the scuffed hardwood floor, and my breath caught in my throat. But the candle sputtered out. Relief coursed through my veins until Cameron bent and lit a page from Grace's journal on fire, a cruel smile twisting his lips. The flame licked at the orange writing hungrily, working its way toward Cameron's fingers.

And then he let go.

Chapter 46

Fire was one of those things I never let myself think about in the after-Grace. I avoided campfires like the plague. The giant fireplace in our house had sat unused after I passed out watching my dad light one of those long matches and lift it toward the hiss of gas leaking from underneath the logs he'd so carefully positioned.

I couldn't smell smoke without thinking about Grace's hair igniting like a firecracker. I couldn't see a spark without picturing the flames engulfing her school uniform. I couldn't feel the burn of a lighter on my fingertips without imagining the skin of her face blistering and peeling in the heat.

Every time I closed my eyes at night, I saw the orange flames licking at my best friend's body. Every time I drifted off into a fitful sleep, I smelled smoke and wondered when fire would finally claim my own life.

Tonight was the night.

The wooden floors ignited as Cameron and Porter shot through the door to freedom. What began as an isolated circle of orange exploded into a room of flames in record time as fire reached toward the ceiling, along the floor, greedily covering every inch of my childhood haven. For a second, I thought about crawling toward the door. I imagined wrapping my sweatshirt around my head and making my way out of this inferno. I thought about saving myself.

But I couldn't see the door anymore and I was tired, so tired of running from Grace's death. The smoke had already filled my lungs. Maybe if I could just rest here for a minute, maybe then I'd be able to determine a way out. But when I rested my head on my arms, I knew I would never get back up. It was time to follow Grace.

"Kate! Kate!" Grace's voice was urgent in my ear. I imagined that she was calling for me. Waiting for me with open arms. But something was wrong. Her voice was shrill and angry. She sounded more like me. "What the hell are you doing, Kate?"

I lifted my head up from my arms.

"Grace?"

Crawl toward the window.

"I can't." My voice was barely a whisper.

You can. Reach your left hand out.

I did what she said and felt the worn molding that lined the walls of her room.

There you go. Now follow that to the door.

"But what about…" The smoke choked my voice.

Go.

Tears stung my eyes and immediately evaporated in the heat. I clung to the baseboard like a rope, clawing my way toward the door. By the time I felt the thin groove of the doorway, I was finally ready to live, to honor the friend that I'd lost.

I reached up blindly for the door handle and hissed in pain when I felt the hot metal scorch the palm of my hand. The fire had spread fast in the abandoned house. Or maybe Cameron and Porter had helped it along. Either way, I knew I'd failed. I was trapped.

"I'm sorry." I wasn't even sure who I was apologizing to anymore. Grace's ghost? My parents? Liam? Honestly, the person I really should have been apologizing to was myself.

And that's when I heard the sirens drifting through the window next to the door. I pulled myself up and pounded as hard as I could on the glass.

"Here! Here! I'm up here!" The glass shattered beneath my fists, but I didn't even feel it slice into the tender skin of my fingers. I only screamed louder in between greedy gulps of fresh air. "Up here! Help! Up here!"

Within seconds, they saw me. Five firemen stood around a huge circle mat begging for me to leap to safety. It should have been terrifying standing on that ledge, the cold night air on my face, the wind lifting strands of hair in a dance. But I wasn't scared. Not for a second. I just closed my eyes and jumped.

Chapter 47

In so many ways, watching Grace's childhood home burn to the ground felt like an ending. Parts of the roof collapsed into her old room, dispersing a puff of bright sparks into the midnight sky as flames scavenged for fuel, roaring and hissing and angry. But as the door to the ambulance slammed shut and my lungs gulped clean oxygen through a plastic mask and Cameron and Porter were hauled away in police cars with flashing lights, I found a beginning.

I just wished it hadn't taken me so long to get there.

"House fire Morningsong Avenue, suspects in custody. One victim, teenage girl, smoke inhalation, first-degree burns, minor lacerations." An EMT radioed the message to the hospital, and I thought of my mom and dad, how pissed they were going to be, how I'd ruined everything again. Another EMT adjusted my mask and squeezed my hand, reading my mind. "You hang in there. Don't be scared. You're safe now and everything's going to be okay."

Everything's going to be okay. Tears gathered at the corners of my wide eyes as I listened to her words, realizing in one gigantic swoosh how long I'd been waiting to hear them. They settled over me like a blanket, and I closed my eyes, relaxed my body, and finally let myself fall asleep.

• • •

Bright white light. Too bright. For a second, I thought there'd been some mistake and I'd actually died, but then my eyes adjusted to mauve speckled wallpaper. Something told me that if there was a God, there was no way he'd allow mauve speckled wallpaper in his heaven.

"Greg! *Greg!*" My mom screamed toward the hallway for my dad, who rushed into the room ashen and stubbly and sad. He clutched at his heart as though his hand resting above it could prevent any further damage.

"What's happened?" he asked, stricken. But then he saw me, saw my half-open eyes, and his face crinkled into the biggest smile I'd ever seen. I searched for signs of disappointment or anger but couldn't find any. My mom's face was lit from within. They weren't mad. In fact, they looked happier than I'd seen them since before Grace died.

"Sweetie. Oh, sweetie." My mom rushed to my side and squeezed my hand, shaking her head back and forth. "You scared us. We're so, so lucky. What would we do without you?" Tears clung to her lashes as she looked to my dad as though he held the answer. His eyes were red and watery.

"Porter? Cameron?"

I couldn't bring myself to ask an actual question.

"In custody. The police are going to have questions, honey. But they made it out and so did you." My mother's voice was matter of fact.

"They hurt…I mean they killed…"

"Shhh…we know. Porter has already told the police everything. You're safe now, and they won't ever come near you again. That's a promise." My father's eyes had a fierceness in them that I'd never seen before.

"They're not well, Kate. At this point, we just have to hope that they're punished to the fullest extent of the law and that they get the help that they need." My mother shot my father a look that meant he should change the subject. Fast.

So he called the doctor in, and my injuries were discussed. I *was* lucky. The burns were minor. I had a few scrapes and bruises, and my lungs would recover. They didn't have to tell me what might have been. We all knew. The reminder hung in the air and settled on each of our shoulders. But instead of slipping backward into the throes of survivor's guilt, into the questions and unfairness that suffocated me after the death of my best friend, I embraced my second chance, thankful that I was out and thankful for everyone who waited so patiently at the other end.

"So the nurses tell me you have some visitors." Dr. Buchanon patted my knee, a warm smile spreading across her face. "It seems that you are one very popular young lady."

My dad gave his patented look—raised eyebrows and surprised frown while nodding the head—and my mom winked at me.

"Are you up for it? Because I can pull some strings and lift the three visitors per patient rule. Or I can send them all packing." She winked.

In a past life, I would have pulled the scratchy blanket to my chin and rolled to my side, shutting out everyone who cared, but in this life, I didn't even consider it.

"I'm up for it," I said, smoothing my hair and sitting up a little straighter.

"Well, you've got yourself a good one, that's for sure. Your boyfriend's been here for hours. Poor thing looked like he'd been hit by a bus. Hang on to him. He's a keeper." *Boyfriend*. Liam? Was he here? A warmth started in my chest and fanned out to my arms, my legs, my cheeks. Over the past eight months, he was the one person who had made it his goal in life to protect me. Everything he'd said, everything he'd done, all of it had one purpose—to save me from myself. I hadn't been ready to see that before, but now after almost dying in a fire, after almost losing him to Bethany, I was finally ready.

My parents made some uncomfortable throat-clearing noises and slipped out after the doctor, explaining that they'd be within shouting distance. I knew that meant they'd have ears to the door, but I didn't care. I kind of wanted to keep them close, as crazy as that might sound.

I sat up straighter in my bed. Craned my neck. Eager to see Liam with my own eyes. Wondering what I'd find when I looked into his.

And in walked Bradley Farrow.

I deflated like a forgotten beach ball.

I'd spent so much of my first year at Pemberly Brown praying Bradley Farrow would notice me or throw me a smile or even slam into me by accident in the hallway. And here he was. But instead of the heart-racing, face-flushing reaction I'd spent first year trying to hide, it had disappeared. In its place was warmth, sure, but not on my cheeks. Yes, he was gorgeous. Yes, I'd discovered how truly amazing he was beneath all the confusion and complication, but he wasn't Liam.

"I know I'm probably the last person you want to see right now, but I came as soon as I heard," he said. "I just…I just wanted to say that it's kind of unfair how life works, and I guess I hope that you of all people might understand that." His golden eyes pierced into mine. "I know everything's all messed up and you blame me…"

"No." I cut him off. "I know now. I know none of this is your fault. Or really anyone's. Nothing is going to bring her back. Nothing." I looked down at the bandages wrapped tightly around my hands.

"You need to know this will never happen again. Truly. The Sisterhood has been disbanded. My dad says they're going to fill in all of the tunnels. It really is over."

You know how sometimes when you get a really bad splinter and it bothers you for days and days until finally somehow you get it out and you feel this crazy rush of relief that the pain is gone? And then right after you're kind of surprised by just how relieved you are, almost like you hadn't realized how much it had hurt in the first place.

That's how it felt, knowing that the societies were finally dead.

Pain that I hadn't fully understood evaporated, and I felt lighter. I held on to the rails of the hospital bed, sure that I was going to float away.

But then I saw the sadness that still creased the lines around Bradley's mouth where his dimples used to be, and I realized he was still stuck at his first beginning. Alistair had just died, and Bradley was still lost in the black cloud of grief, trying to find his way out without his best friend. Despair tightened my chest just thinking about what lay ahead for him—the long, bleak process of trying to figure out a way to live your life with a chunk of your heart missing. I could only hope that maybe he'd learn something from me. And who knows, maybe I'd actually be able to help him on his way.

"I need you." The words sounded broken, discordant coming from Bradley's mouth. "I mean, I need a friend." He spoke to the floor as though he were ashamed to need help, to not be able to do this alone. "And I can't think of anyone who could possibly be the friend I need right now. I can't think of anyone…" he lifted his eyes to meet mine, his lashes like fans, "but you."

The tears caught me off guard. I wasn't much of a crier, never had been, hopefully never would be. But once they started, I couldn't turn them off again. They ran down my cheeks in their narrow rivers, the drops falling to my lap and darkening the blanket.

I nodded as I swiped them away, new streams replacing the old. Nodded and sniffled and cried even harder when Bradley rushed forward for a hug. I could use all the friends I could get. I realized that now. And there was no shame in depending on other people. I couldn't possibly do this alone, and neither could Bradley. And right then, we had each other.

"I guess I should go," Bradley said, pulling away. He smiled then, and it took me back to first year when my heart about burst out of my chest at that smile. Something told me that a guy with a smile like that was going to be okay. I mean, how could he not be? "You have, like, a million people out there, and you know how Pemberly Brown feels about waiting." We laughed then as I wiped away my remaining tears, and Bradley waved good-bye.

Chapter 48

The door flew open, and a body barreled right into Bradley, like a fly smashing into a windshield.

"What the…"

"Language! We're in a hospital," Seth joked, waggling a finger at Bradley. His eyes were still red from crying, but Seth was completely oblivious, as usual. His slapped red cheeks matched his flaming hair, and he charged at me like a mini-comet. His bony arms dug into my body as he did his best to wrap me in some kind of bear hug. I grimaced at the pain of a few tender spots, and he jumped back as though he'd been scalded.

"Oh geez, I'm sorry! Did I hurt you? Oh Kate! A fire? How did this happen? I'll kill them! Are you okay? Will you be okay? Why didn't you call me?" He would have continued, the questions spilling from between his lips, if I hadn't raised my hands to defend myself from the ginger inquisition.

"Seth, I'm fine. Really, I'm fine."

"I didn't mean to interrupt, I'm sorry." He appeared even more flustered and then stood and rushed back to the door. "Oh my gosh, I forgot Maddie!" He poked his head into the hallway and called her name, waving her toward the room. Voices spilled in from the hallway, and I wondered how many kids from school were out there. I wondered if Liam was among them. I couldn't believe they had come.

I knew I looked like complete shit, but when Maddie walked in, I realized I was in good company. Her hair was pulled into an unruly mess at the top of her head, and her eyes were bloodshot and ringed in red. Her cheeks might have been as puffy as my own. As soon as she saw me, she burst into tears.

She cried through words I couldn't make out, but I knew Maddie well enough to understand that she was saying sorry and thank you and I miss you and everything's okay and most importantly, *we're* okay. We'd returned to a new beginning and were given another chance to start over and learn how to be friends again. And this time, I wasn't going to let what happened to Grace hold us back. This time, I really was ready to let all of the tears wash our slate clean and get my best friend back.

"It's okay, it really is. We're going to be fine." I whispered the words into Maddie's shoulder, and for the first time, I really believed them.

She pulled away and stared into my face, lip trembling.

"I'm not sure how to tell you this…"

Her words made my heart race. Was it Liam? God, I knew there had to be a reason he wasn't here.

"I'm sort of in love with Seth." She whispered the words, her cheeks as red as his hair.

Because I'm a horrible, selfish person, my first reaction was relief. Thank God her big reveal had nothing to do with Liam. But I mentally kicked myself in the ass. *I mean, really, Kate? Your best friend professes her love for your other best friend, and relief is the best you can do?*

And then it came. Happiness. A smile that was so big that I thought my face was going to break in half. Seth beamed from behind her, and I matched it. We all did.

A constant stream of students poured into the room, which was exhausting and exhilarating at the same time, if that's even possible. But as I watched Seth and Maddie giggle together and hold hands and flirt, I couldn't stop the tiny pulls on my heart.

Seth elbowed Maddie and raised his eyebrows toward me. "Overwhelmed yet?"

I tried to appear thankful. "Oh my gosh, yes! I can't believe all these people. It's crazy. I didn't even know anyone knew who I was."

"Everyone loves you, Kate. You should see Amicus. There are pages and pages of messages. Teachers, parents, students, even Mr. Bob the custodian. It's crazy!"

We both knew what I was thinking, but I couldn't bring myself to ask where Liam was. I wasn't ready for the answer, wasn't ready to hear that it wouldn't work between us, that it never could, that it was my fault he'd been expelled from Pemberly Brown.

"But we should let you sleep. You're probably exhausted," Seth said, standing. Both he and Maddie gave much gentler hugs this time and closed the door gently behind them. And it was so quiet then, too quiet.

"Mom?" I shouted toward the door. "Dad?" The door remained shut, and I deflated into the sheets, sinking down and feeling sorry for myself.

I couldn't believe that I'd been stupid enough to think that Liam might show up. He must hate me after all I'd put him through. I tried to get comfortable despite the tubes, and when the door opened a few minutes later, my face lit up. But it was only a nurse coming to take my vitals. I turned to my side and faced the window, back to the door, eyes closed, and tried to convince myself Liam's absence was for the best. We weren't meant to be. Our timing sucked.

And then the door clicked quietly, and although I'd never understand how I knew it was Liam before I even rolled over, I knew he had finally come.

Chapter 49

I heard his sharp intake of breath before he approached the bed, and I wondered what it might mean. Was he still angry with me? Had he come to tell me he never wanted to see me again?

I kept my eyes closed and my breathing even. Turns out after all this waiting around, I wasn't quite ready to face him yet. I knew I had to apologize, but I had no idea how. Easier to keep my eyes closed a little longer. At least with my eyes closed, there was a chance that he might stop hating me. And right then, I'd rather have a chance than the truth.

Laundry detergent followed Liam wherever he went. I always joked that he had to have the cleanest clothes of anyone at PB, and it was no different now. I loved the way he smelled, like fabric softener and Tide. God, I really didn't want to spend the rest of my life without that smell.

He placed his palm on the side of my head like it was always meant to be there, smoothing my hair lightly. It didn't feel like the touch of someone who was planning on leaving.

His breath caught and his hand shook a little, tiny noises escaping in puffs of air, and I realized he was crying.

"Kate," he whispered.

I squeezed my eyes shut. It sounded like he loved me, but what if I had my signals crossed? What if he was just trying to be a good friend? Trying to forgive me for being so awful? I focused on making my breathing slow and steady.

"I've been watching everyone come in and trying to figure out what to say to you, because even though I shouldn't be, I'm so mad." His words were barely audible, a confession more than anything else. He was here, but he was angry. "You just keep doing this. You keep self-destructing. It's killing me."

I accidentally forgot to breathe, and Liam paused.

"You can turn over now." There was a smile in his voice, so I risked cracking open one eye, then two, and then rolling to my other side…Liam.

I felt like I was seeing him again for the first time. Faded navy T-shirt, hair curling over his ears and down the back of his neck, his eyes blue instead of green today. And yeah, he was hot. Super hot.

But it was more than that. So much more. His mouth twisted up into a half smile. The corners of his eyes crinkled as he brushed his hand across my forehead, smoothing my faded neon red hair out of my eyes.

"Hi." He still had that funny half smile, but his eyes were serious. Drinking me in.

"Hi." My eyes didn't leave his. I felt like I could stare at him for days. Maybe if I looked at him long enough, hard enough, he'd understand how much I loved him and how sorry I was for what I put him through. Maybe I wouldn't have to say it, because I knew whatever slipped out of my mouth would never be good enough.

"Look, I'm not even sure you want me to be here right now."

I do.

"You scared the shit out of me, Kate."

I know.

"I'm sure you're going to need time to work through this, to figure everything out, but it's just getting too difficult to be around you like this."

No. Please, no.

"I just want you to be happy."

Yeah, right.

"So, I guess I'll leave you to it. Please just take care of yourself, okay? I couldn't…I just, I hate to see you hurt."

Too late.

Liam hesitated for a second but finally stood and began walking to the door.

I watched his fingers grip the handle. I watched him pull it open. I almost let him leave.

Almost.

"I love you. And I'm sorry. I'm so, so sorry."

The words were thick and foreign on my tongue, one on top of the other. I wasn't even sure if they were intelligible.

But Liam must have understood, because he was back at my bedside before I could say anything else.

"You what?"

"I'm sorry. It was all my fault you got kicked out of school, and I tried to do everything I could to fix it…"

"No, not that." He waved his hand. "The charges were dropped. I'm back in." Liam walked back over to the bed. "The first part."

"I love you?"

His lips were on mine before I could finish. His hands tangled in my hair, my fingers wrapped around his neck, and we kissed. This is going to sound totally cheesy, but he took a piece of me with that kiss. Or maybe I finally just gave it to him.

He pulled away after a minute and tipped my chin so our eyes could meet.

"I love you, Kate." I was close enough to see the flecks of blue and green and brown in his eyes, the flecks that always made them change color on a whim. Today, more than anything else, I saw truth swimming between the swirling colors.

"I love you too."

Chapter 50

I guess I shouldn't have been surprised to see Grace's journal sitting on top of my desk when I finally returned home from the hospital. I shouldn't have shivered when I ran my fingers over her name etched into the bright pink cover using an orange pen.

I have no idea who left it there for me. Probably Porter or Cameron. But my heart wanted to believe it was Grace.

I thought about opening it up. I thought about reading every word. But instead I walked over to my closet, ballet flats clicking and creaking on the wood floor, and pulled down the brown cardboard box on the top shelf. It was covered in dust, and I felt a sneeze tickling my nose as I balanced the weight in my arms.

I slid off the lid of the box, my fingers catching on the rough edges of the cardboard. The snapshots and notes and slam books were all jumbled together, and I carefully picked up my favorite picture, the one with Maddie and Grace that we took before upper school started, before the world swallowed up our childhood. Our faces were soft and dimpled, our eyes sparkling with possibility. Hope. I unfolded the frame and placed it gently on my nightstand. I wanted to remember the way we'd been, because I was ready to start being the person I'd become. But there was nothing wrong with a little hope.

I carefully lifted Grace's pearls from around my neck and snapped them into the large velvet box that Ms. Lee had presented me with after Grace's funeral. I loved the pearls, and I'd miss their cool reassurance on my neck, but it was time to retire them. Maybe someday I'd wear them again. Someday when they reminded me of something other than revenge.

I lifted the journal from my desk and stacked it carefully on top in the box. The pages felt heavy with secrets, and part of me wanted to devour them all. But a bigger part of me knew that I needed to let Grace go. I was happy to have her words, her thoughts nearby. But that didn't mean I had to read them. Dead or alive, every girl deserves to keep some secrets.

Besides, I had different plans for today. My bruises had mostly faded, and I had that familiar itch that always came with big changes in my life. Thankfully I planned for such occasions, and I had just the thing to scratch it.

I flipped open the small closet next to my bathroom and started digging around for some hair dye. The past seventy-two hours had changed my life. I felt different, so it was only fair that I look different too.

It wasn't easy to find the right box. I had a few stockpiled, a rainbow of colors I figured I'd need at some point. I felt my lips turn up in a smile when I finally uncovered the right color behind the packages of purple and platinum, blue and green. I ran my fingers over the model on the box, so pretty and happy, like she held the secret to it all. I could use a secret like that.

Because I'd changed. I was never going to be the Kate who rode her bike to the drugstore with her two best friends and stayed up all night laughing and eating Twizzlers. I was never going to be that girl in the picture, but I was ready to go back to being me. Well, the new and improved me, that is.

As I rinsed the dye from my hair, I let a few other things slip down the drain as well. Regret, guilt, revenge, sadness. I'd reserve the right to feel these things occasionally, but I desperately clung to hope instead. Because hope was what moved you forward.

Chapter 51

T he secretary did a double take as I signed my name on her clipboard, her thin lips turning up in a smirk. I'd dyed my hair enough times to grow accustomed to the extra attention, but I couldn't help but smooth the soft strands anyway, returning her smile as I took my seat.

Half a beat-up-looking magazine later, she ushered me into the familiar room where Dr. Prozac was typing something into his computer, his back turned to me. For some reason, anticipation bubbled in my stomach. Dr. Prozac was right up there when it came to people who would care about the color of my hair, and I had to admit I was excited for him to see my new look. My appearance was a hot topic of discussion during our sessions, and I couldn't wait to hear what he might conclude about my latest choice.

He turned around, and I waited for it…waited for it…and then, a flick of the eyebrows, wide eyes, blinking, and finally a smile.

"Kate!" He clapped his hands together, his face warm and alive.

It was kind of a shocking reaction from a normally very composed person. I couldn't help but laugh.

I lifted a chunk of hair near my face. "Natural."

"It suits you." Dr. Prozac nodded to the ass-numbing chair and I took my usual seat.

I was finally back.

Chapter 52

From Grace Lee's Journal—September 13

Tonight's the night. The bonfire. I've tried on about a million different outfits. Turns out it's kind of tricky to know what to wear when your life is about to change.

Change. God, sometimes I'm not sure I'm ready for this. I know the societies are important. I know we need to come together as one, but lately when I look at Maddie and Kate, I'm tempted to warn them. Maybe if I told them the truth, we'd laugh at how stupid the societies are and everything would go back to the way it used to be.

The truth is, I liked our middle-grade bubble. I loved riding bikes and staying up all night watching scary movies and writing our deepest, darkest secrets into a puff-painted notebook. I miss it. All of it. Especially my friends.

I just wish there was a way to stop time. To stop everything. I know that probably makes me sound like a baby, but it's the truth. The problem is that you can't stop time. You can't stop change. Change is coming. Change is here. No more hiding behind Kate.

Oh, I hope they'll understand. I hope they'll be proud.

Last night, I had a dream that there was an earthquake on campus. And it was horrible. The ground shook and cracked, a huge fissure divided our school in half. I remember looking at the ground split into a cliff and seeing Maddie and Kate on the other side.

I woke up crying.

I hope that if tonight causes an earthquake, it will push us together instead of splitting us apart. I hope they'll forgive me.

Acknowledgments

A huge thank-you to our incredible editor, Leah Hultenschmidt, who knows exactly when to replace an exotic, private island getaway with sleepover camp. And to the rest of our fabulous Sourcebooks family—especially Jillian Bergsma, Cat Clyne, and the awesome publicity team—for taking such good care of our babies. Kate and the entire Liar Society gang have been in good hands.

We couldn't do any of this without our agent, Catherine Drayton. Her guidance, advice, support, and one-liners are imperative to our survival. Plus, she's always right, and that helps too.

The Liar Society series will always have a special place in our hearts, and we hope we've done right by Kate. Thank you to our family and friends for believing in us and her.

About the Authors

Lisa and Laura Roecker are sisters turned writing partners with a passion for good books, pop culture, and Bravo programming. Not necessarily in that order. Lisa has always been a phenomenal liar and Laura loves to write angsty poetry, so writing for young adults seemed like a natural fit. The sisters live in Cleveland, Ohio, in separate residences. Their husbands wouldn't agree to a duplex. Visit www.theliarsociety.com to find out more.